MONSTROUS TALES – VOLUME 3
Long reads for late nights

I0551755

Edited by Dorothy Davies

MONSTROUS TALES – VOLUME 3
Long reads for late nights

GRAVESTONE PRESS

TABLE OF CONTENTS

All Hail the Melon Heads

Edward R. Rosick

It was raining stones.

Not little pebbles but big fuckers, baseball sized, large enough that if one hit you in the head it would be a bloody mess at best, lights out permanently at worst.

"Fuck!" DJ yelled, clutching his left ear. "I'm hit, E, I'm hit!"

"Get closer to me." I was cowering under a small oak tree so I pulled him tight alongside me. I wanted to see if Weasel, Hot-Rod and Monique were faring any better but I didn't dare stick my head out.

"Where are the rocks coming from?" DJ asked. Blood was running down the side of his skinny neck onto his frayed Detroit Lions pullover.

"I don't know," I replied, but deep down, I was afraid I did know. We had found whatever was haunting the grounds of the asylum. Or more accurately, it—or *they*— had found us.

***

It had started like most things—DJ and Weasel, two of my best friends at Lincoln Park High School, arguing, this time about the nuances of the latest video game they were addicted to. We were at Council Point Park on the banks of the sluggish

Ecorse River, pounding down some tall boys on an early Friday afternoon in late October, waiting for our two other friends, Hot Rod and Lee, to arrive. It was just about a perfect autumn day in southeast Michigan—some high clouds but mostly sunny, temps in the low 60s, leaves on the trees in full change sporting brilliant colors of yellow, orange and red.

"What do you say, E?" Weasel asked.

"About what?"

DJ waved dismissively at Weasel. "About the stupid shit that's coming out of his mouth." Although he was dressed almost the same as Weasel except for a Detroit Red Wings hoodie, they would never be mistaken for blood brothers. DJ was five-eleven, about my height, with long, greasy black hair tied up in a haphazard man-bun, overweight round face, small eyes and lips so red they looked like he wore lipstick. Weasel was five six, one-twenty soaking wet, sharp nose and chin, with spiked light brown hair already receding.

"All I said was that Hank Greenberg was the greatest athlete to ever play in Detroit," Weasel said. "Everybody should know that."

DJ shook his head. "No, scrotum-face—everybody knows that Stevie Yzerman was the greatest."

"Sorry," I said. "I'd have to put my money on Barry Sanders."

"He didn't play for the Tigers," Weasel said.

"Or the Red Wings," DJ added.

I sighed and looked for another tall boy in our cooler. It was empty. "Yeah, you boys got me there." I stood up and arched my back, causing several pops to echo in the air. "It's almost time for fifth hour. We should be getting back. It doesn't look like Hot Rod and Lee are joining us."

Weasel laughed. "Yeah, right. Like we're going back to school."

"I mean it," I said. "Fifth hour is trigonometry and I'm getting a solid C. Graduation is eight months away and I don't want to fuck it up."

"Relax—we're all gonna graduate," DJ said. "Who the hell doesn't graduate LP High?"

"You two, if you don't start going to class."

"Thanks for your concern, *Dad*, but me and Weasel have world history fifth hour," DJ said. "Why the hell do we have ti learn about dead people?"

"Yeah," Weasel said, "what's the use learning about shit like that?"

Sometimes I just never know when to shut up. "Did you ever hear the saying 'those that forget the past are doomed to repeat it?'"

DJ and Weasel both looked at me like I was speaking ancient Egyptian.

"You spend too much time reading, E," DJ finally said, before lighting a fat blunt. "Did you ever hear the saying, 'Friday is high-day?'"

DJ and Weasel laughed while I dug around in my pocket for car keys. I almost wished I had lost them, since they were paired with my 2009 Chevy Impala, a true Detroit POS if there ever was one. I'd paid fifteen hundred dollars for it the previous spring and had put in at least that amount in repairs since then. Every time I parked, I prayed to the car gods that somebody would steal it so I could collect the insurance money.

"What are we gonna do this weekend?" DJ said between tokes of the joint.

"Monique said she'd like to go to a haunted house or something like that," Weasel said.

"We should go to a haunted house on Halloween," DJ opined. "That would be dope."

"Halloween night is the Ecorse-LP football game. Winner of it goes to districts," I said.

"Then there's no way I'm going to a haunted house that night," Weasel said. "Monique would kill me." He passed the blunt back to DJ and stood up. "I gotta go piss. Be right back."

"But I need to get back to—" I started to say, but Weasel was already booking to the outhouse. I sat down next to DJ.

He passed me the blunt and I shook him off. "I don't like weed, DJ. You know that."

"That's weird, dog." He took a long hit then blew out a stream of perfectly formed smoke rings. "You'd be a lot less anxious if you smoked."

"Thanks for the advice, doctor," I said sarcastically. I wished DJ was correct; if weed could chill me out like other people, I'd be a somewhat happier maladjusted teenager. But all it did was make my anxiety and paranoia worse. My drugs of choice were alcohol and benzodiazepines, particularly Xanax. With a bottle of Strohs and a handful of xannies, I could face the world with a fake smile on my face.

"I bet Weasel is talking to Monique," DJ said.

I nodded. Weasel and Monique Shoniqua Brown, she the star of the track and girls' basketball team, leader of the high school band, and probable valedictorian, were the unlikeliest couple at LP High. Weasel was going out with a six foot, one hundred and seventy pound—none of it fat—girl with skin so dark it was almost ebony. I had heard her described as a Nubian princess and it fit perfectly.

He had been bragging for the last month that he was having sex with her and, like all things Weasel, I blew it off as just more bombastic bullshit until the night of our home football game with Melvindale. My Impala had broken down yet again and I was in the far field of the high school which functioned as a spill-over parking lot during home games. In the light of a full-moon, I spied Monique's silver 2015 BMW X5 and noticed the rear door was open, which I figured meant she was around. I walked over the back of the car, intending to bum a ride, but instead saw a sight that is forever burned into my brain cells: Monique naked and on all fours, her back arched in orgasmic pleasure and Weasel, wearing only a Bob Marley t-shirt , pounding her from behind like a horny jackrabbit. A few seconds later he grunted like an angry steer then rolled onto the floor, his pale skin slick with sweat. Monique finally relaxed and looked over her shoulder at me. "You mind shutting the damn door?" she said, unperturbed.

I shut the damn door and walked the mile and a half back to my house.

"You boys miss me?" Me and DJ turned to see Weasel walking back.

"No," DJ answered. "What took you so long?"

"I wasn't gone that long."

"Talking to your honey?" DJ asked.

"As a matter of fact, I was." Weasel grabbed the smoldering roach from DJ's fingers and killed it off with two long puffs. "She said she missed her little Snowball." He laughed. "That's what she calls me—her little Snowball."

"Maybe it's because of your little pee-stick," DJ said.

Weasel grabbed his crotch. "This stick fills her up just fine," he said, then flicked out his over-sized tongue like a lizard tasting the air. "And this never fails to get her off."

"That's gross, man."

"Monique doesn't think so. And speaking of dick-sizing, you're one to talk, DJ. We've all seen your little wee-wee."

"It was cold that day in gym class, okay?"

But Weasel was right. DJ had been cursed with LDS—little dick syndrome—and he hated to be reminded of it.

"Did you talk to Monique about going to a haunted house?" I asked, to diffuse the tension.

"Yeah. She said she'd think about it."

"I know," DJ said. "We could go hunting at old man Wertman's. Pheasant season opened yesterday."

"No way," I said firmly. Wertman was a mean-ass Methuselah who lived on 160 acres south of

12

Jackson, a friend of a cousin of a friend of DJ's dad. "I had a nightmare about that guy."

Weasel frowned. "About old man Wertman?"

"It was crazy. I dreamt that all of us went hunting on his property and DJ blew Lee's head off with a shotgun."

"Damn," DJ said. "Why'd I do that?"

"I don't know. All I remember is we were trying to figure out what to do with Lee's body and then Old Man Wertman shot all of us."

"He shot you?" Weasel said. "I thought when you died in a dream you like, died for real."

"He shot all of us, but I was the only one he didn't kill. I think I ended up killing him but that part is fuzzy."

"You probably dreamed that from all the horror movies you watch with Weasel," DJ said. "You should stick to porn; then you'll just have kick-ass sex dreams like me!"

"I'm living my porn dream," Weasel said, "and her name is Monique Shoniqua Brown."

I grabbed the cooler. "And I want to fulfill my dream of graduating high school, so I'm heading back."

"You're such a buzz-kill," DJ groused.

"But I'm a buzz-kill with a car," I said, "so unless you two want to hoof it back to school, quit whining and get to stepping."

***

Later that day and after much debate, we settled on going to a haunted house. For some reason—

13

mainly my inherent laziness—I agreed to let DJ search online to find one, because Weasel said he and Monica were going off to play, quote, "hide the Weasel willy."

The next morning was another beautiful autumn day—blue skies, sixty-plus degree temps and a light southerly wind. Because of that and also because I was tired of staying at my dad's place and dealing with his new twenty-eight year old airhead girlfriend walking around the house in lace panties and my dad's wife-beater t-shirt, I decided to walk the half-mile to DJ's house, where we would be picked up by Hot-Rod.

The trek was mostly peaceful through working-class blocks filled with towering oak and maple trees, kids playing soccer and football in the streets and old people (anyone over thirty) raking their leaves listening to everything from college football to rap music.

It was a small change, turning off of Outer Drive onto Eighth Street, but the scene immediately changed. DJ's house, a small, three bedroom Cape Cod with a one-car garage was across the street from one of Lincoln Park's mobile home parks, or as it was better known, the meth factory. Three times the previous summer when we were drinking beer out in his garage, muffled explosions from the park informed us that yet another amateur *Breaking Bad*-wannabe chemist had learned too late that watching television shows does not count as Ph.D. chemistry training.

To my surprise—since getting up before 1 p.m. on the weekend was anathema to my stoner friend—DJ was sitting on the curb in front of his house, furiously tapping away on his new iPhone.

"Hey, DJ," I said.

He looked up at me, frowning, then back down to his phone. "Hey, E."

"What are you doing outside?"

"The twins were driving me crazy."

"They're eight years old and you're their big brother. That's what they're supposed to do."

"Lucky me." Every few seconds his phone would ping, prompting him to type out some answer.

"Who are you texting?" I asked.

"Some asshole. He's driving me crazy."

"Who is it?"

"I don't know," DJ said in an exasperated voice, "but when I find out I'm definitely kicking his ass!"

smiled. DJ talked a great game of being a tough guy, but a fighter he wasn't.

"Maybe you should just block him and call it a day."

"Fuck that. This asshole started it and I'm sure as hell gonna end it."

So it went for another five minutes. Ping-text-ping-text-ping-text.

I finally grabbed the phone out of his hand. "Let me see if I can figure out who this is." The pinging immediately stopped.

"Ha!" DJ said in triumph. "I showed that dickhead! Just when you take it he quits texting."

n my short seventeen years on this planet, I have come to believe two immutable truths: the only thing constant is change and there are no coincidences.

I quickly scrolled back through the texts and saw they were the same, that is,

if DJ texted **U R an asshole!** the 'other' would text **U R an asshole!** When DJ would text **Why U copy me?** his texting doppelganger would text the same message.

"You're texting yourself," I said.

"What?"

I gave him the phone. "Look at the phone number. That's your number that you sent to me two days ago when you got your new phone. You told me you switched carriers, right?"

"Yeah. When I got the new phone."

"That's it. You forgot you got a new number and you're just texting yourself."

He shrugged and put the phone in his pocket. "Well, everyone can make a mistake, right?"

I nodded and wondered if he had any beer in the garage.

"Why'd you walk?" DJ asked. "The Impala go POS on you again?"

"Yep."

"Bummer, man."

"No surprise. But it was good to get out of my old man's house and walk to clear my head."

"He giving you grief again about your school grades?"

"No It's his new girlfriend."

"Latisha, the tall Hispanic chick?"

16

"Nah, they split already. This one's a white Goth chick named Candy, or Bambi, or something like that. She mumbles so I can't understand her most of the time."

I sat on the curb next to DJ and continued. "I try not to judge him about dating these honeys who are half his age, especially since he and my mom were sleeping in different bedrooms the last three years they were married. But damn, walking into the bathroom this morning and finding a big purple butt plug floating in the sink filled with dirty water… I just don't need that scene."

"That's nasty. Was it hers or his?"

"I didn't ask."

DJ kicked at loose asphalt in the road. "You think we're gonna be like that when we're old?"

"I've no idea what I'm going to be like when I'm eighteen, much less *old*."

Sounds of jazz music hit my ears; I looked up to see Hot-Rod rolling up in his classic rebuilt '69 Plymouth Barracuda. I nudged DJ and we walked to the car, where I saw Weasel and Monique in the back seat, wearing jeans and matching LP HIGH MARCHING BAND hoodies.

"Sweet music," I said to Hot Rod through the open driver side window. "Who is it?"

Hot Rod smiled, a Hollywood-white grin in a face that movie buffs like myself likened to a young Wesley Snipes. He had on a pair of dark-tined Ray-Ban sunglasses, a black US Marines sweatshirt and matching black jeans. "Art Pepper. One of the all-time greats."

17

"Too bad he's a white guy," Monique said from the back seat. "There's a million great black jazz musicians, but Marvin here has to be playing music from a white guy."

"He plays a bad-ass sax," Hot Rod said, "so I could give two shits what his skin color is."

Monique shook her head and looked out the window.

"And by the way," Hot Rod said, "I do not like going by Marvin, so if it pleases your Highness, call me Hot Rod or get out of my car."

"Damn, who's on the rag today?" Monique said. "Fine, *Hot Rod*. Is that better, *Hot Rod*?" She turned to Weasel. "Now tell me true—what kind of name is Hot Rod for a brother?"

Weasel went to speak, looked at Hot Rod staring him down from the rear view mirror, turned to Monique, then tapped on Hot Rod's shoulder. "Can you open the door so I can go into DJ's house to take a piss?"

"We're not done with this conversation," Monique called as Weasel scampered away.

"Where's Lee?" I asked Hot Rod.

"Had to work all day. Apparently big show at GlamorGirls tonight." He pointed at me. "How 'bout you? Don't you usually work Saturdays?"

"I quit."

"You quit a fine culinary establishment like White Castle?"

"I know. Hard to believe, right?"

"Didn't you quit last month?" DJ asked.

"I did but then went back. Then quit again."

"Damn," DJ said. "I was diggin' getting free gut-busters."

"Sorry to be a buzz-kill about your free food, but I'm tired of smelling like steamed meat and onions."

Hot Rod laughed. "Don't worry, DJ. E will be back there. He's a masochist like the rest of us."

DJ raised his eyebrows. "Damn, E, didn't know you swung that way but hey, it's all good, I mean, if you like doin' the deed with fat old transexuals, then—"

"DJ, shut the hell up," Hot Rod said. "It's too damn early to be hearing your stupidity."

"What?" DJ said indignantly. "I'm just tryin' to be all accepting and open-minded like we learned about last week in our inclusiveness class. I'm just saying if E likes—"

"DJ!" The volume and tone of Hot Rod's voice left no room for debate. DJ sheepishly stepped away from the car, pulled out a dime bag of weed and began rolling a joint.

"What are you doing?" Hot Rod asked.

DJ looked at Hot Rod, looked down at the joint, then back at Hot Rod. "I'm rolling a joint."

"Why? You know you're allowed to smoke in my car."

"I know that," DJ said, "I'm not stupid, you know. I'm getting it ready for when we get to the haunted house. You know, chill out a little before we get the shit scared out of us."

"You're sure this place is open?" I asked.

"Like I just told Hot-Rod, I-ain't-stupid. Of course it's open—why would I pick out a haunted house that wasn't open?"

"Fine," said Hot Rod, "although it would have been nice if it hadn't been an hour away in Ann Arbor."

"It's actually between Ann Arbor and Ypsilanti," DJ said, putting the cigar-sized blunt in the pocket of a red and black flannel shirt he was wearing. "I got the directions all up here—" He tapped his head, which sounded like a woodpecker feeding on a hollow tree—"so don't even need to map it out on my phone."

"Map out what on your phone?" Me and DJ turned to see Weasel on the sidewalk.

"Where you hide your balls," DJ said.

Weasel grabbed his crotch. "They're right here for you to be jealous of."

"Get your big balls in the car, Snowball," Monique said, pulling Weasel down to the car and giving him a deep kiss.

DJ looked at me, rolled his eyes and went to sit in the front bucket seat before I loudly cleared my throat.

"What are doing?" I asked him.

"What the hell is with y'all this morning and your questions? I'm getting in the car, dog."

"That's my seat," I said. "That's always been my seat and always will be my seat."

"Aw, c'mon," DJ said. "That's not fair."

"DJ, what have I told about life and fairness?" Hot Rod said, like a father asking his child.

DJ's chin dropped to his chest. "That life's not fair."

"Exactly," I said, pulling up the front seat so DJ could get in back to sit next to Weasel, who was occupying the middle. "Now let's go and get the shit scared out of us."

***

The haunted house—more specifically per the large, neon sign just off the road, MICHIGAN'S MOST TERRIFYING, HORRIFYING, BLOOD-SOAKED TERROR-HOUSE!—looked the part. It was a three story brick farmhouse straight out of the eighteen hundreds, a large, rickety appearing wooden porch bathed in gallons of blood and animal entrails leading to a massive oak door. Multiple darkened windows adorned the front of first and second stories, while the third story had a solitary picture window just below a crumbling turret made of black slate tile.

Unfortunately, it was also closed until sundown. Again, per the large neon sign.

"You gotta be fucking kidding me." Hot Rod turned around, glaring at DJ. "I thought you said you checked to see if it was open."

"I did!" DJ said. "Their website said it was open all weekend."

"Did you happen to check the times it was open?" I asked.

DJ looked at me, at Hot Rod, at me. "They said they were open all weekend! I mean, hell, it's close

21

to Halloween—what haunted house is closed so close to Halloween?"

Hot Rod sighed loudly. "All right—what's plan B?"

The car was uneasily quiet for a moment before Monique spoke up. "Are y'all up for a *real* haunted place?"

"Sure," Weasel said, not hesitating. I have no doubt that would have been his response if she said. 'Are y'all up to getting pushed through a wood chipper?'

"What are you talking about?" Hot Rod asked.

"There's this impressive old psychiatric hospital, built over a century ago, just outside Manchester," Monique said. "It's been abandoned since the 90's when the state starting shutting down all the asylums. There's been talk since then of tearing it down, or turning it into a hotel, but as far as I know, it's still just a creepy, abandoned and what I've heard, *haunted* building."

"How do you know about it?" I asked.

"My grandfather was one of the first black psychiatrists in Michigan. I remember him telling me stories about working there in the 1960s and 70s."

"Damn, that's way back," DJ exclaimed. "I didn't know they even had hospitals then."

"Eight years, ago, before he passed away, my grandfather drove me out to see it," Monique continued, ignoring DJ. "It was right about the same time of year as now. I remember how macabre the place looked—broken windows, a section of it burned down, overgrown brush and trees

22

surrounded it… when my granddad told me of ghosts of former patients haunting the halls, it was easy to believe."

"I got nothing better to do this afternoon," said Hot Rod, "so someone map out the directions and let's go find us some ghosts."

***

Ghosts roaming its halls or not, Monique wasn't kidding when she called the Manchester State Psychiatric Hospital an impressive building. We arrived there thirty minutes later on a narrow, two lane asphalt road a couple of miles off the main drag. Thick layers of grey nimbostratus clouds darkened the early afternoon sky and cast shadows across the cracked and faded face of the five story brick building. The main structure was almost a quarter mile long with staggered wings branching out to either side like the arms of a monster bat. The roof held multiple ornate spires, part of the state-of-the-art ventilation system per Monique, at least back in the day.

"It took over eight million bricks to make this place," Monique said like a well-versed travel guide, "from the Crooked Lake brickyard twenty miles away, all of them carried in carts pulled by mules. Today this place would take at least a couple decades to finish; back then, three years."

"That's very informative," Hot Rod said. "Did they put up the fence then too?"

23

He was referring to the eight foot high fence topped with tangled bundles of razor wire around the entire hospital perimeter.

"Don't worry, pretty boy, there's a back service road that me and my grandfather used. It'll take us to a gate that's not fenced and locked."

"Uh huh," Hot Rod grunted. "How far down?"

"A ways. Just keep driving. But slow."

"Hey, you didn't tell us about the Melon Heads!" It was DJ, face buried in his iPhone.

I turned around. "The what?"

He jammed the phone in my face. "Melon Heads—deformed little cannibal monsters that live in woods and tunnels around the hospital."

Monique snatched the phone from him like a rattlesnake striking a mouse. DJ glared at her but said nothing.

"There's been numerous reports since the nineteen-sixties of small, humanoid creatures with massive heads that have a taste for human flesh in the woods and underground tunnels surrounding the Manchester Psychiatric Hospital in southern Michigan," Monique read. "Some people claim that these beings, called Melon Heads by the locals, are the results of cold-war genetic CIA experiments on children who were orphaned and left at the hospital."

"How come it's always the CIA that does these bad things?" DJ said. "I bet it was the Russians who did it."

"You don't think our government wouldn't ever fuck with us common folk?" Monique said, sarcasm lacing her voice.

24

"I don't know. I mean, they got a lot of other stuff to worry about, like climate change, and—" DJ stopped, looked at me then back at Monique—"the Russians."

"Haven't you heard of the Tuskegee study?" Monique asked.

DJ's brows furrowed in concentration before his eyes lit up. "Yeah! That's where this big-ass meteor hit Russia a long time ago, right?"

"You're thinking of the Tunguska event," I corrected him.

"Yeah, that's what I mean. The Tunguska event. Where this big-ass meteor hit Russia and started World War One," DJ said proudly.

Monique shook her head. "DJ, you're the dumbest white boy I ever met. The Tuskegee study was when the US government, from 1932 to 1972, did a study on syphilis among 600 black men in Alabama. 'Course, all the study did was watch these poor black men die horrible deaths from the disease without treating them."

"Damn," DJ exclaimed. "That shit really happen?"

"Yeah," I said, "that shit really happened."

"Well, that was like forever ago," DJ said. "Things are a lot different now."

"Bullshit," Monique said with conviction. "Back in the 1990s the government, *our* government, tested an experimental measles vaccine on poor black and Latinx kids in Los Angeles, a vaccine that was shown to cause an increased death rate."

25

DJ pursed his lips. "Now that one I'm not buying. Our own government pushing experimental vaccines on kids? That's definitely a crazy conspiracy theory."

"It's the damn truth," Monique said angrily. "Listen—at the end of the day, people in charge, in the government—people who get off on controlling other people—don't change and if they do, it's only for the worse."

Hot Rod loudly cleared his throat, then said "sorry to break up your deep discussion back there, but it looks to me like the road is ending and I don't see any gate."

I peered out the windows. To our left, visible through scrub oak and brambles, was the hulking shell of the mental hospital; to our right was an overgrown field and, straight ahead, the road seemingly ended more overgrown brush.

"No, it's right up there," Monique said.

"The road *ends*," Hot Rod countered. "You want me to just smash through the brush? This is a classic '69 Barracuda, not some 2-ton Hummer."

"I'm telling, you, that's it." Monique pointed to the front. "Humor me. Just drive up to the end."

Hot Rod sighed and slowly drove up to the end of the visible road, then turned off the car. "Okay. Now what?"

"Now we go see a haunted hospital."

Hot Rod opened his door, but before anyone got out, Weasel tapped Monique on the leg. "So, baby, what about those Melon Heads? I mean, did your grandfather know anything about them?"

She shook her head. "Ain't no such things. Just more internet bullshit."

"But what if it's true internet bullshit?" Weasel asked.

Monique pinched Weasel's cheeked and laughed. "Then I guess they'll be chowing on some skinny-boy white meat tonight!"

After getting out of the car, we followed Monique. "Look," she said triumphantly, pointing to a gate barely visible through the brush. She pushed her way through the scrub and brambles, unhitched the gate and pushed it open.

"What's that you say, Hot-Rod?" Monique said. "You just say, "damn, Monique, you were right again?"

Hot Rod kept quiet before going through the gate, the rest of us quickly following.

Knee-high grass and weeds covered the ground leading to the hospital, along with broken beer bottles and pop cans, evidence of other people coming to see another crumbling building from Michigan's glorious past.

"Stop," DJ said. "I wanna record this." He took a few steps away from us and panned back and forth with his new phone.

"The cameras on this new iPhone are so bitching!" he said. "Too bad I didn't have it this summer when we caught that mermaid in Lake Michigan."

Monique turned to DJ. "What'd you say?"

"I said that we caught a mermaid this summer."

"We?" Weasel said indignantly. "What's with this 'we' shit? I'm the one that brought her in."

"Yeah, with me and E helping you," DJ said. "If it wasn't for us, that mermaid would've pulled you into Lake Michigan and ate you for her midnight snack."

"You boys can't be serious," Monique said, looking at Weasel, then at DJ. "You saying you actually caught some mythical creature out of Lake Michigan?"

"Wasn't anything mythical about it," DJ said. "Right, E?"

It felt weird as hell agreeing with DJ, but I did.

Monique shook her head. "You white boys are the craziest motherfuckers I've ever met." She turned to Hot-Rod. "What the hell is a good-looking brother like you hangin' with these crazy motherfuckers?"

Hot Rod shrugged. "Somebody has to watch their ass. Might as well be me."

"I'm good-looking too, right, baby?" asked Weasel.

Monique laughed, grabbed his face, and kissed him hard. "'Course you're good-looking," she said after pulling away. "At least for a skinny little white boy!" She laughed again while making her way toward the hospital.

Weasel looked at me, eyebrows scrunched with confusion. I patted him on the shoulder and moved us toward the building.

Monique led us around the front of the building to the back, where a rusted steel door was partially open.

"How the hell did you know we could get in this way?" Hot Rod asked.

"I didn't," said Monique. "But I *did* remember my granddad telling me that sometimes the staff would leave this door open—against rules of course—so that they could go outside to get their WAP filled."

Since I was in front, I opened the door and stepped inside onto a cracked concrete floor in a large, dimly lit landing. Going up and down were stairs leading to more doors.

I turned to Monique. "Which way?"

"Up. You don't wanna go downstairs."

"Why not?" It was DJ, standing next to me, taking pics with his phone. "What's there? That where they store the bodies?"

Monique sighed. "No, that's not where they store the bodies. It leads to work tunnels that run all around the complex. My granddad said they hadn't been used in years. By now they're probably full of sewer water and rats and other nasty shit."

I grabbed DJ's arm and pulled him up the stairs. "C'mon—I'm sure there's more than enough for you to take pictures of without wading in sewer water."

We entered the ground floor, a long hallway off to our right and a shorter one to our left that ended in two massive wooden doors leading to the front entrance. Acrid smells of rodent piss, stale air and mold hung heavy in the air. I tried to breathe through my mouth as much as I could. Dim light from side windows—some busted open, some still intact—illuminated walls covered in yellowing, peeled paint that looked like skin coming off the corpse of an ancient giant. The plaster behind the

29

paint was adorned with a copious amount of graffiti, proclaiming such philosophical axioms as

SUK MY BBC

I LOOOOV CAMDEN J

WE'RE ALL GONNA DYE!!!

"This is great!" DJ gushed, the flash on his phone lighting up like a strobe light as he took picture after picture. "Once I put this shit up on my YouTube Channel I'm gonna get thousands of likes."

"No, you're not," said Monique, stepping in front of him.

DJ frowned. "What you talkin' 'bout, girl? Don't be dissin' on my—"

"DJ, if you keep trying to talk like a black man I'm gonna knock you out," she said with no trace of humor in her voice.

DJ stepped back and wisely remained silent.

Monique cleared her throat, then continued. "What I mean is what we're doing is illegal. If you put any pics up online and some tight-ass gets it in their mind to turn us in to the po-pos for breaking and entering, my chances of getting a full scholarship to Harvard or Yale are done. You wouldn't want that, would you?"

"No," DJ answered quickly.

"Good." Monique smiled and slapped DJ on the cheek, light enough not to leave a mark but hard enough to send the sound echoing down the hall. "Now take all the pictures you want, sugar. Just make sure they *stay* on your phone."

We walked down the long hallway, peaking into rooms, some filled with boxes holding decaying clothes and mice-chewed papers, others as empty as ancient tombs.

"What was this floor used for?" Hot Rod asked Monique.

"Intake of patients and administration." She pointed to one room on our left with a high ceiling of at least ten feet holding only one small window, rusted iron bars covering it still present. "That was where they put patients who were, as my grandfather said, 'not amenable' to being here, to cool down."

"What if they didn't cool down?" DJ asked.

Monique grimly smiled. "They all cooled down. One way or another, they all cooled down."

"So what's up in the other floors?" asked Weasel.

She bent down and kissed him on the top of his head. "Aww, isn't that nice—you being all inquisitive and such." She stretched out her arm like a tour guide giving a lecture. "On the second floor we have more offices as well as the cafeteria and rec room and main security office. The third and fourth floors were patient rooms—third for women, fourth for men. The fifth floor was reserved for those patients who needed more intense treatment."

"You mean the really bug-fuck crazies, right?" DJ said with total sincerity.

"Yeah, if you want to be crass about it," Monique said.

DJ looked at me. "What? They weren't bug-fuck crazy?"

31

I pulled on his arm as we all headed up the stairs to the second floor. "C'mon, Mr. Sensitive, let's get you on another floor to take more pictures."

The second floor looked pretty much the same as the first, except for a couple of larger areas used for food service and recreation. After meandering around for a few minutes, we headed up to the third floor to check out the patient rooms.

The stairwell opened into a short T-shaped hallway, one longer end blocked by a heavy door with a small wire-meshed double window high up on the thick oak.

"The next three floors have this layout," Monique said. "This area is where the nurses, doctors and security all stayed. Through the door are patient rooms."

She pulled on Weasel's hand toward the staff rooms. "I want to see if I can find my grandfather's office."

"Let's go check out the patient rooms," Hot Rod said to me and DJ, but DJ shook his head.

"I wanna take some pics in here, then I'll join you two," he said, already snapping photos.

Like all the other doors we had encountered, the one to the patient side was unlocked. As Hot Rod and myself made my way down the empty corridor, I noticed the walls had no paint, just dull grey cinder blocks sans any graffiti.

"Why you think no one has written anything up here?" I asked Hot Rod.

"I don't know. Maybe they have and the ghosts cleaned it up."

"Ha ha. Very funny but wrong. Everyone knows ghosts don't give two shits about graffiti."

We walked the halls; it felt different up there. Colder, quieter, our footsteps no longer echoing, the sound somehow being absorbed by the walls and the high ceiling. It was like a forced silence, brought about by the decades of pain and suffering from those who had been locked inside this building.

All in all, it was downright creepy.

"Damn, E, if you weren't crazy when they brought you in here you'd be after being locked up in one of these rooms," Hot Rod said. He was standing in a patient room and, after making sure the door couldn't lock behind us, I followed him.

The room was small, six by eight feet, with dull gray cinderblock walls and was devoid of any furnishings except the shattered remains of a toilet on one end of the room. Like the rest of the building so far the ceiling was high, at least ten feet, with one small square window at the top letting in a few meager rays of dim sunlight.

We walked the rest of the hallway to another set of thick double doors. All the rooms were pretty much the same.

"Now what?" I said. "I would imagine that the women's floor is just as depressing as this one."

"Let's go to the fifth floor," Hot Rod said.

I hesitated. "I don't know. I'm already bummed out by looking at what the patients down here had to deal with."

"C'mon. Don't be a pussy."

"I'm not a pussy. It's just that—" I shrugged— "with my fucked up psyche, I probably would have been put in a place like this if I lived back in the day."

"We *all* would have. But so what? You know what my old man says about ifs."

"If pigs had wings we'd all be covered in pig-shit," we said in unison and laughed before heading up the stairs to the fifth floor.

With the sun obscured by clouds, there was hardly any light on the final floor of the hospital. Long shadows filled the hallway and both Hot Rod and myself turned on the flashlights on our phones.

"Should have brought real flashlights," he said.

"No argument from me." We peered into the first couple rooms we came across. They were tiny, like enlarged closets with no windows, dark concrete cubicles that must have heard decades of unhinged screams.

"Damn," Hot Rod said, "these rooms would be even small for someone the size of Weasel."

"Maybe they had a height and weight restriction to get up here."

"I doubt it." We moved on and came to a steel door hanging off rusted hinges to our left. Hot Rod pulled it open, revealing a short hallway.

"What the hell is this?" I said.

Hot Rod put up his phone to provide illumination. "Let's find out."

I followed him in. The air was colder, denser, like walking into an old meat locker. Down the short hallway to the right there was another high-ceiled room but unlike the patient rooms, this was more spacious, it held a thick, rectangular ceramic tub bolted to the middle of the floor. The ivory sides were stained brown and rust red. I hoped it was from hard water and not blood. On both ends were rusted shackles to hold wrists and ankles.

"Interesting place to take a bath," I said. Hot Rod said nothing, just stared at the tub. I noticed his hands were shaking.

"What is it?" I asked, never having seen my friend so shaken.

He sighed and ran one hand through his short black hair. "Did I ever tell you the story about my mom's Uncle Emil?"

"No."

He turned off his phone light and looked at me. "You know that she escaped from East Germany when she was a little kid, right?"

"Yes."

"It was really due to what happened to Uncle Emil that her and her dad took the huge risk to leave. After the communists took over and set up their police-state, my mom's dad, Rudolph, got this low-level position in the Stasi, the East German secret police. My mom said he wasn't proud of what he did, but it was for his family—his wife and my mom—and I guess he figured he could at least protect them if he was on the inside."

Hot Rod sat on the edge of the tub for a few seconds, then apparently thought better of it and stood back up. "Anyway, Uncle Emil, Rudolph's brother, was crazy mad at this and started working with the underground to overturn the government."

"That sounds like a bad idea."

35

Hot Rod nodded. "Uncle Emil was arrested and taken to one of their mental hospitals, although they weren't really hospitals at all. They were prisons."

I looked at the shackles on the tub and shuddered as Hot Rod continued.

"I heard the story once from my mom when I was a kid, when some cousins came over from Germany to visit. She told me how my grandpa Rudolph had to identify Emil's body. The prison officials said he had had a heart attack while taking a bath. Grandpa Rudolph had found him in a tube like this—shackled, his head two inches below the water, close enough to see the ceiling but deep enough to drown." Hot Rod shook his head. "Imagine finding your only brother drowned in two inches of water."

I stepped back from the tub, visualizing some poor soul being held down, unable to breathe, all because of what they believed.

"I guess that's what drove my grandpa Rudolph to really see the rotten, evil system he was part of, when he started planning on how he could get his family out of East Germany so they all didn't end up like his brother."

Hot Rod became quiet for a moment, then spoke again. "You hear shit from your parents when you're a kid and it doesn't mean anything. You're a kid and all that grown-up shit is just that, grown-up *shit*, and you never think it'll mean anything to you. But seeing this, thinking of my Uncle Emil, thinking of my grandpa Rudolph and my mom and what they must have been going through... kinda shows me why my mom has the political convictions she has."

"Let's go find the others," I said, wanting to get myself and Hot Rod away from this room. We both turned to leave when a high pitched sound, not really a scream but more than a yell, broke the silence.

"Reeeeeeee!" is the closest I can describe it, like something from the mouth of a tortured animal.

Or a really pissed-off ghost.

"Reeeeeeee!" the sound repeated. We both ran out of the room, me in front by a half a step and if my bladder had been more full I'm sure I would have pissed my pants, because on the far end of the long hallway, bathed by the shadows, I saw a figure dart across the floor. It was only for a second, but the thing was short and misshapen, with long skinny arms and wobbly legs and skin that appeared almost translucent in the shifting shadows. I didn't even see where it went—down the stairs, into a room, although I couldn't remember any rooms at that end of the wall, or, even though I refused to believe the possibility, into and through the wall.

"Did you see that?" I whispered to Hot Rod.

He nodded. "Yeah. I saw it. What the hell was it?"

We looked at each other a split second before another scream, this one even higher pitched, broke the silence.

"You believe in ghosts?" he asked me.

"I didn't until now."

I'm ashamed to say that I think I did dribble in my shorts when I felt a hand fall on my back. I know I screamed and jumped back into Hot Rod, almost knocking him down.

It was Weasel, standing next to Monique. "What are you screaming for, E?" he said.

I restrained myself from punching him. "Shit, Weasel, you trying to give me a heart attack?"

"Sorry," he said sheepishly. "I thought you heard us coming up."

"You two see anything strange?" Hot Rod asked.

"Like what?" Monique said.

"I don't know. Just... strange."

Monique and Weasel looked at each other before Monique answered. "I saw something out on the grounds when I was in my grandfather's old office. It looked like two or three people, or at least things."

"Why do you say two or three?" I asked.

Monique frowned. "It was weird. One second I thought I saw three figures running through the tall weeds, but then one of them just seemed to disappear."

"It's ghosts," Weasel proclaimed, as if it was the most natural fact in the world. "They do disappearing shit like that."

Monique shook her head. "They weren't ghosts, sugar."

"I don't want to be contrary," Weasel said, "but then how in the hell did one disappear?"

I finally noticed something and asked, "Where's DJ?"

"I thought he came up here with you," Weasel answered.

"I thought he was downstairs with y'all," said Hot Rod.

"We split up," Monique said. "He was annoying the shit out of me taking pictures of every damn thing with his phone."

I peered down the darkening hallway. "You think that shape we saw was him?"

"Making that sound?" asked Hot Rod, "or down the hall?"

"Both."

"You probably saw a ghost," Weasel said.

Monique, hands on hips, starred down at Weasel. "What did I just tell you? There are no damn ghosts. It was probably your idiot friend, DJ, with the shadows making him appear all weird and—"

"Hey guys!" a voice yelled from the other end of the hall. It was DJ, running like he had a rabid Rottweiler on his ass.

He skidded to a stop next to Hot Rod. "It was total nightmare action down there!" DJ said, panting. "Total nightmare action!"

"Down where?" I asked.

"In the tunnels." When Monique glared at him he put up his hands. "I knew you and Weasel wanted some alone time and I figured E and Hot Rod had the upstairs covered, so…"

"Did you see a ghost?" Weasel asked. "We did."

Monique grabbed Weasel's shoulders and shook him. "Baby, if you say that one more time I'm gonna slap your lips off."

39

DJ held out his camera. "I don't know what I saw, but I got a picture of it."

We all looked at the phone. On the screen was a picture of crumbling brick walls, tangled wiring hanging from the ceiling, and a figure—short, pale to the point of almost being translucent—just outside the full flash radius, but enough so that its eyes—bulging in a large misshapen—glared in the light.

"Sure as hell looks like a gho—"Weasel swallowed the last part of the word and looked up at Monique. Fortunately for him she didn't slap his lips off his face.

"What'd you think it is?" DJ said.

"Something weird," Hot Rod answered. "*Real* weird."

"What was it like down there?" I asked DJ.

"Creepy. Cold, damp. Smelled like our gym locker room on a hot day. But it's not flooded or anything."

Weasel tugged on Monique's hand. "Let's go check it out."

Her face scrunched in disgust. "Into those nasty tunnels? No way."

"I'm with Monique," DJ said. "While it would be cool to get some more ghost pics, I'm down to leave. *Now.*"

"Never thought I would hear myself saying this," Hot Rod said, "but I'm in full agreement with DJ."

I wasn't about to argue—there was no way I wanted to go down into the tunnels, ghosts or not—

so I followed the rest downstairs to the first floor. I was never so happy when we followed DJ outside.

Until we realized we had come through the wrong door.

Which of course locked solid behind us.

"Where the hell are we?" Hot Rod said, looking left to right at weeds, brambles and stunted oak trees.

Monique sighed. "We're in the courtyard. It's where they'd let patients get some sun, have some smokes, shit like that."

"That was awful nice of them," Hot Rod said. "They do this before or after they tortured them?"

"What the hell you talking about?" Monique shot back.

"Me and E saw some nasty shit on the fifth floor. Looked straight out of the Soviet gulag."

"I have no idea what you're talking about, but if you're implying my grandfather was part of that, you better watch your mouth," Monique said, getting chest to chest with Hot Rod. "Your tough guy image would fall way down when people found out I kicked your ass."

"Call your girlfriend off, Weasel," Hot Rod said, his voice deadly quiet. "The only reason she isn't on her ass right now is 'cause I don't lay hands on women."

"Fuck you," Monique said. "I don't need no man to tell me what to do." Both her hands shot out and slammed into Hot Rod's chest. He staggered back and would have fallen if I hadn't caught him.

"I mean it, Weasel," Hot Rod said, "call this crazy bitch off or—"

41

I heard a sound like a hammer hitting a coconut a split second before Weasel cried out and rubbed the back of his head.

"What the hell?" Monique said. "What happened, sugar?"

"Something hit me in the head."

"Probably a bird taking a big dump," DJ opined.

Weasel flipped him off. "It wasn't a bird, numb-nuts. It felt like a rock."

It was a rock, because a few seconds later more came flying at us, a shower of misshapen stones. They weren't little pebbles but big fuckers, some even baseball sized, large enough to that if one hit you square in the face or head it would leave a bloody mess at best, lights out permanently at worst.

"Fuck!" DJ yelled, clutching his left ear. "I'm hit, E! I'm hit!"

I looked around; a ten foot tall oak tree was just to our right, so I grabbed DJ and pulled him over to get at least some protection from the stony missiles. Hot Rod, Weasel and Monique took off the opposite way.

"Where the hell are those rocks coming from?" DJ said. There was blood running down the side of his pale neck.

"I don't know," I said, but deep down, I was afraid I did know. We had found whatever was haunting the grounds of hospital. Or more accurately, it—or *they*— had found us.

The attack continued for another minute— although it felt like an hour—and then stopped. I poked my head around the tree to see if I could figure out who was responsible. All I saw was weeds and a few gnarly-limbed trees.

"Hey E—is DJ alive?" It was Hot Rod calling from somewhere to the left of me.

"I'm bleeding pretty bad!" DJ yelled out before I had a chance to answer.

"His ear is sliced open but he'll live," I said while DJ scowled at me. "Where are you guys at?"

"There's a couple fallen trees at your 9 o'clock about 40 feet away. There's room for you and DJ to come over."

"I think we should just stay here," DJ said. "I've lost too much blood to move."

"You're gonna be fine," I said, not really knowing if that was true but not knowing what else to say. "Besides, haven't you heard the saying 'there's safety in numbers?'"

"I bet the person who said that wasn't bleeding to death."

"Probably not. Let's go anyway." I grabbed DJ's arm and half-dragged him to my left through the weeds, brambles tearing at my clothes and face. I expected any second to feel a stone turning my skull into a busted pumpkin, but there was no further attack.

"I think I'm gonna faint," DJ said when we got to Hot Rod, Weasel and Monique. They were crouched under a pair of rotting oaks that had formed a rough x-shape, the middle providing somewhat of a shelter from a rock barrage.

"Damn, boy, your ear is cut up like a piece of cafeteria lunch meat," Monique said to DJ.

"I told you!" he said to me in an accusatory tone. "I *am* dying!"

Monique shook her head. "You aren't dying." She took off her faded blue LP High hoodie and wrapped it around DJ's head. "There. That should stop the bleeding."

DJ glared at me before lying down. "Glad at least someone cares about me."

"Isn't that gonna ruin your hoodkie?" Weasel said to Monique.

"So what? I'm a track star. I can get all the hoodies I want."

"Anyone have an idea where those rocks came from?" Hot Rod said. "I'd like to get out of this place before the sun sets – with my skull intact."

Monique pointed to her right. "There's—or there used to be—an open area with some picnic tables and such for the patients. That's where I think whoever was throwing the rocks were."

Hot Rod nudged me on the shoulder.

"C'mon, E. Let's go see if we can knock some sense into those assholes who busted open DJ."

"What if there's more taen a couple of 'em?"

"Then we'll have to kick a few more asses."

"Since when do you two get to play the macho heroes?" Monique said. "If you go we all go."

I have no desire to play the macho hero at all I thought, but kept silent.

Monique pinched Weasel on the cheek and shook it. "C'mon, let's see who's fucking with us."

"Maybe it is better if only Hot Rod and E go," Weasel said. "DJ's probably still woozy from blood loss—" at this, DJ groaned and grabbed his head—

"so one of us needs to stay here with him and if you stay then I'll have to stay and—"

"Both of you," Monique said to Weasel and DJ as Hot Rod moved out, me close behind. "Get your white asses in gear and move!"

The sun was low on the horizon, hid behind the crumbling escarpments of the hospital, long shadows filling the inner sanctum. No more rocks rained down but my heart beat wildly as I plowed through the waist-high weeds behind Hot Rod, making enough noise for an eighty-year old deaf man to hear.

Hot Rod threw up his right hand in a fist and I stopped, only to be run into by DJ.

"Damn!" he yelled, grabbing his head. "Why'd you stop like that? I think I split open my ear some more."

"Shut the hell up," Hot Rod said, peering out over the weeds. I crept up beside him and I damn near yelled myself.

Monique was correct about the open spot. Thirty feet in front of us was an area the size of a basketball court, with over-turned and busted up picnic tables and rotted wooden chairs littering the gravel-covered ground. Standing among the remains of the tables and chairs were half-dozen creatures.

They weren't ghosts or goblins, but definitely the strangest looking humans I had ever seen. They stood, at most, three and a half feet tall. All had deformed hydrocephalic heads, with wrinkled faces holding bulging eyes, flat noses and ears almost too small to be seen. A couple of them were bald, three others had white, wispy hair that fell to the shoulder

45

and one, the tallest of the bunch, had on a long black wig, the synthetic hair reaching almost to the ground. They wore layers of tattered clothing that looked as if it hadn't been washed since the 1960s.

Hot Rod and I squatted back down. He looked at me, started to speak, then shook his head and remained quiet.

"What is it?" Weasel excitedly asked. "Did you see some real ghosts?"

"Not ghosts," I answered, "but I think we found the Melon Heads that DJ told us about."

Weasel's face dropped. "Really? Aren't they cannibals?"

"I gotta get a pic of them," DJ whispered, then popped up like a whack-a-mole, phone camera in hand.

Hot Rod pulled DJ down. "Get your ass back down here. If they see us and start throwing rocks, we got nowhere to hide."

"Then we better think of someplace to hide real fast," DJ said, "'cause I think they saw me."

A couple of seconds later a high-pitched chattering, like monkeys in a rainforest, along with a few Reeeeees! we had heard in the asylum, came from the Melon Head group.

"What are they doing?" Weasel said.

"Sounds like they're talking, or what passes for Melon Head speech," Monique answered.

"Maybe they're calling out to us," DJ said. "Maybe they want something."

Hot Rod frowned. "What the hell could they want from us?"

"Maybe they want us to worship them," Weasel said. "I saw this movie a couple weeks ago called Crimson Biker Bloodbath. In it, these bikers came across some mutants in the desert who wanted to be worshiped like gods."

"So what do we do?" said DJ. "Kneel in front of them and start chanting 'all hail the Melon Heads?'"

Weasel shrugged. "Couldn't hurt to try."

"I think one of those rocks hit your damn head, Snowball," Monique said.

"I think we should *quietly* go back the way we came and try some other door and get out of here," I offered.

"Best idea I've heard all day," Hot Rod said, right before the Melon Head chattering stopped and rocks starting raining down on us again.

"We're gonna die!" DJ cried, curling up into a tight ball.

"Cover your heads," Hot Rod said, as a stone clipped my elbow, sending sharp pains into my shoulder and hand.

"Fuck!" Monique yelled. I looked over and saw that she had been hit on the side of her face, blood already flowing.

"Baby, you're bleeding!" Weasel said and then, in what I can only guess was a case of testosterone and love-fueled rage, grabbed the baseball sized rock that hit Monique, stood up, and threw it with all his might at the Melon Heads.

There was a sharp, cat-like cry and the barrage of stones suddenly stopped. I slowly pulled my hands away from my head and looked up at Weasel, who was still standing.

"What happened?"

"I think I hit one."

"And?" Monique said.

"Uhh…y'all need to look," Weasel said.

The rest of us stood next to Weasel. In the clearing, five of the Melon Heads were circled around the sixth, the shortest one with white hair, now stained red with blood. All of them were crying like wounded cats.

"I didn't mean to hurt it," Weasel said.

"I just wanted them to stop throwing rocks at us."

"They were trying to kill us," DJ said. "Ain't no need to get apologetic."

At the sound of DJ's voice the Melon Heads turned toward us and, while part of me agreed with DJ, another part could feel Weasel's shame. Half of them were crying, fat tears streaming down their filthy misshapen faces and all were gibbering at us, almost as if explaining their previous actions.

"I think they just wanted us to leave them alone," Monique said. "Maybe they were throwing rocks at us to scare us away."

"Maybe they should have just told us to leave," DJ said.

"And maybe you'll realize they can't talk," Monique shot back.

"Oh. Yeah. That would definitely make it hard for them to tell us to leave."

"Let's get the hell out of here while we can," Hot Rod said.

All of us—sans Monique—agreed. She stood with an inscrutable look on her face, starring at the Melon Heads.

"Damnit," she finally said, "I can't leave 'em like that." She wiped the blood out of her eyes, then proceeded to walk directly over to the group.

"Baby, what are you doing!" Weasel cried. "Don't go over there! They're cannibals!"

"They're *not* cannibals," I said.

"How do you know?" Weasel countered. "When was the last time you saw a cannibal?"

Hot Rod shook his head. "What the hell is that girl doing?"

Monique was standing in front of the group of Melon Heads, who still circled their wounded comrade.

"It's okay," she said, her voice calm and serene. The Melon Heads looked at her with cocked head like inquisitive dogs. "I just wanna see your friend, okay?" She motioned with her hand and spoke again, this time too quiet for us to clearly hear.

"Do you think she can speak Melon Head?" DJ asked in awe.

"It wouldn't surprise me," Weasel answered. "She's fluent in Spanish, French and Arabic—why not Melon Head?"

Whatever she said—in Melon Head or not—the group of five let her in. Monique parted the hair of the wounded Melon Head and even from where we were, we could see the gash was deep and bleeding freely. Monique stepped back and peeled off the black long-sleeved t-shirt she was wearing, revealing her toned abs and dark red lace bra. She

49

folded the t-shirt into a makeshift wound wrap, which she expertly placed on the bleeding Melon Head. The creature smiled, revealing three yellowing teeth, and gently patted Monique on the arm. Another Melon Head, the one wearing the long black wig, also smiled then pulled down his ragged pants, revealing a misshapen but absolutely huge, erect cock.

"What the hell?" Weasel said. "That damn Melon Head wants to tap my girlfriend!"

The black wig Melon Head took a step toward Monique. She slapped his woodie—hard—with a sharp flick of her wrist.

"Oww!" we all said in union and the Melon Heads, at least the male ones, copied us. Black wig Melon Head yelped and jumped back. His penis shrank like a punctured balloon and he stuffed his shriveled member back into his dirty pants, looking down like a chastised little boy.

Monique adjusted the wrap, then came back to us, the Melon Heads watching as if she was an angel sent from heaven.

"That was awesome!" Weasel gushed.

"What part?" she asked. "When I dressed the wound or slapped down that wood?"

"Dressing the wound," Weasel immediately replied. "I mean, you had every right to slap that dick, but…"

Monique laughed and kissed Weasel on the head. "Don't worry, Snowball—I only do that to naughty boys."

"So what do we do now?" I asked. "Do we call the po-pos, or—"

"Call them about what?" Monique interrupted.

I frowned. "About the half-dozen mutant Melon Heads we found at an insane asylum."

"We're not calling anybody." Monique said this as a proclamation of fact.

Weasel grunted. "I don't understand. We can't just leave 'em here—" he pointed to the Melon Heads, who apparently had now lost interest in us and were playfully tearing up weeds and throwing them at one another—"with winter coming."

"They've survived other winters," Monique said.

I looked over at the Melon Heads, cachectic, old and bent over like wind-ravaged trees, clothes tattered and torn. "I don't think they'll make another winter."

Monique put hands on hips and looked at me. "E, I know you're supposed to be the smart one of your posse, but think—if we call the po-pos, what will happen?"

I pondered the question for a few seconds, then shrugged. "I don't know. Guess they'll take them somewhere."

"Yeah, they'll take them somewhere all right. To some research facility to poke and prod and see what the hell made them the way they are. In short, they'll be treated like freaks."

"They kinda are freaks," DJ said.

"They're *people*," Monique said," just like us. And like all people, they want their freedom and to be treated with dignity and respect, two things they *won't* get if we call the cops."

"Then what do we do?" Weasel asked.

51

"We leave," Monique said to him. "Next week, you and me will bring some clothes and food and leave it in the tunnels, I bet that's where they're living."

We all looked at one another, then to the Melon Heads, who were still happily tossing weeds at one another, gibbering nonsensically in their high-pitched voices. I still didn't feel right leaving them here, alone and facing another brutal Michigan winter, but Monique had a point; if they were taken by the authorities, their lives would go from precarious to horrible.

"She's right," Hot Rod proclaimed. He turned to her and smiled. "This might be the only time you'll hear me say this, but I was wrong earlier; you're not a crazy bitch. You're a woman who can see things the way they are, even if sometimes that way is a hard way."

"Thanks, Hot Rod," she said, smiling back. "Now let's go home."

Miraculously, we found a door that wasn't locked, made our way through the darkened asylum to the front door and quickly walked to the car.

"Damn—that was the best haunted house ever!" DJ exclaimed. "I mean, except for almost getting killed by rocks thrown by the Melon Heads and all."

"You sure you don't need to go the emergency room?" Weasel asked Monique, who told him in no uncertain terms that a superficial cut on the head was not going to land her in a hospital.

"I just don't want it to get infected," Weasel continued." It's so close to your brain and all."

Monique shook her head and laughed. "Snowball, if you didn't have such a talented tongue, I'd send you packing right now."

"That's way too much information," Hot Rod said as we got to the Barracuda.

"Don't be a hater, Hot Rod," Monique said, then laughed again.

"I hang with knucklehead white boys," Hot Rod said. "I think that proves big time that I'm definitely not a hater."

Monique smiled. "I guess it does. Maybe when I become president of the United States I'll make you my civil rights commissioner."

"What about me?" Weasel asked in total sincerity as we all got in the car.

"Don't you worry, baby," Monique said. "I got big plans for you too."

The sun had set and a full moon was rising over the eastern horizon when we pulled away from the hospital. The car was filled with talk about Melon Heads and Halloween and the big football game with Ecorse the following week. I even managed to push away my ever-present anxieties and let myself get caught up in the camaraderie, enjoyed the feeling of being a seventeen year old who, like all seventeen-year olds living in a rich western country, never gave one thought about death and dying even as the Melon Heads were probably facing their last days. The world and our lives felt like they would stretch out forever on that night in October of 2019, but as we were all to learn in a few short months, things could—and would—change in ways that none of us could ever imagine.

One Long Hot Deadly Month of Summer

SJ Townend

"Typo?" Sam called out from the fridge.

"A typo? An additional, entirely fabricated month? You're off your rocker. It's knocked all the other dates out of sync. Rest of the year is a write-off." Ralph tossed the spiral-bound calendar onto the sofa, on top of the plastic wrapping from which he'd just unsheathed it."My birthday is meant to be on a Saturday this year, not a Tuesday."

"Help me give the shelves a wipe before I load it up, will you?" Sam was kneeling on the tatty laminate flooring of the kitchenette. "This place isn't as clean as I'd hoped. There's... sticky black feathers everywhere. Gross stringy gloop all over the salad tray. God, this stuff stinks of stale death." Sam stood, mock wretched, and wrung his jay cloth in the sink before returning to degreasing the crisper drawer. His husband continued to sulk.

"What a waste of money," Ralph said, arms folded, eyes throwing daggers at his purchase.

"We'll go back tomorrow and get our money back, after a good night's sleep. It's just a calendar."

"S'pose so."

"You've got one on your phone anyway. I don't understand why you wanted that one so much."

"I thought it'd be nice to tack up on the wall whilst we're here, and back home. A souvenir. It's got nice photos of beach sunsets in it. The shopkeeper said there were pictures of fossils in it too, from the digs along the bay. I thought that would interest you. Plus, I guess the old bag was a sharp saleswoman."

Ralph fetched his faulty souvenir and thumbed through its pages again, searching for the additional month. He flipped over July. There it was, 'Beachtember', with its thirty-one additional days, accompanied by a large photograph of a semi-excavated Apatosaurus fossil, slotted in right after July, right before August. His heart skipped a beat as he studied the image. Had the photograph of the old thunder lizard skeleton just furled its upper lip, revealed its dagger sharp teeth, winked at him with a blood-red eye?

"I mean, seriously, 'Beachtember'? If they're going to mess with paying customers and prank tourists like this, they could at least come up with a better name," Ralph muttered, choosing to ignore what he thought he'd seen. He slumped back into the dusty faux-leather recliner. "Can't believe that old crone conned us out of 150 pesos. Imagine if it *hadn't* been half price..."

"Love, let it go. I'm guessing it was half price as we're already half way through the year. Who buys calendars in July? Speaking of which, this summer's whizzing by, isn't it? I can't believe it'll be August tomorrow."

"Not according to this calendar it isn't. It'll be bloody 'Beachtember'. Wonder if I can find the

'Bonus Kiosk' on Trip Advisor. Might leave a bad review." Ralph dug into his pocket for his phone. "Bet it's not on the net—it all seems a tad backwards round here."

"Language, Ralph."

"Oh come on, I don't mean an actual bet—it's a figure of speech, Christ. Idiot."

"Lighten up, Ralph. Please. Put your phone away. The doctor said to minimise stress. 'Digital detox'—work on reconnecting with your higher self. It's the only way you'll silence your demons."

"No bars anyway." Ralph hurled his phone on top of the calendar. "Booking accommodation without Wi-Fi was not your best idea."

"There's plenty to do here without the internet. We can laze in the sun, walk, swim, search for nearby digs, hire a *fotingo*, head into the city to find some rumba. What we're not going to do though, mister, is keep on grumbling. We're not going to spend every evening online ignoring each other and we're not going to think about gambling."

***

The following morning after coffee, Ralph picked up the faulty calendar, wrapped it in his beach towel and slid it into his rucksack.

"It's roasting. You could've picked an apartment with air-con. I can feel my sun block sliding off."

"Ralph. Please. Can we do today with positivity, even if you have to fake it? It's not all about you—this is my holiday too."

56

"Don't I bloody know it..."

"Ralph!"

"...I'd have chosen somewhere a little less focused on digging up old bits of crap from the ground and a little more lively, for sure. This place is a graveyard. There isn't even a bar here."

Sam's eyes began to well up. "You don't have to get involved with the digs."

"Surely there's *something* left of the inheritance. A few pesos to put us up somewhere more... refined... air-conditioned?"

Sam unscrewed his water, glugged half of it back then rammed the bottle hard into his bag before dabbing away pearls of sweat from his brow. He snapped. "Funnily enough, after paying off your sizeable gambling debts, there wasn't enough left for butler service and five star accommodation."

Old Aunt Elysium, whom Sam hadn't seen since he'd been small, had left him a couple of thousand in her will—just a squeeze more than they'd needed to clear some rather threatening illicit arrears Ralph had acquired. There'd been enough left over to get them both out of the city for summer. Sam had taken the opportunity to book a trip to the place he'd so often lectured his palaeontology students about but had never visited and figured the break might also help Ralph with his addiction.

"Why don't you flog that revolting ring she left you as well? Free up more capital. Treat us to an upgrade, some cooler air?" said Ralph, mentioning not for the first time the ugly piece of jewellery Sam's aunt had also bequeathed him.

"You know I can't sell the ring, her will specifically said to keep it—for good luck."

The ring was made from blackened metal and bore a miniature bird skull with two embedded red rubies for eyes. It fitted Sam's pinky perfectly, although he'd never wear it out of the house.

"It's disgusting, Sam. You and I both know that."

"I've packed sandwiches for breakfast. Egg and tomato, extra salt, just how you like it," said Sam, desperate to lighten the mood.

"Thanks," Ralph grunted.

"Come on, let's check out the beach."

***

They made their way down the never-ending, trampled path which broke between a jungle of six foot tropical grasses. The rubble eventually merged into hot, white sand which stretched either side as far as the eye could see. The sun beat down on their fair skin from a ceiling of perfect azure sky above.

"Think I'm going to keep these on," Sam said, waving his flip flops, hopping as his feet screamed with the heat of the sand.

"I need some new ones," said Ralph. "Any chance of some cash?"

Sam looked directly at his partner. "If I give you cash—"

"You don't need to say that," Ralph interrupted. "I don't need a lot anyway—sandals, water and crisps. It'll save you coming shopping with me."

"Are you sure?" Sam's eyes widened, seeded with doubt.

"Sam, come on. There's nowhere here to gamble anyway. The place is dead."

He spoke the truth. The white sands stretched sideways as far as the eye could see and not a dinghy or a soul was out on the flat ocean. All that could be seen was nature of blue and white and green, apart from the small shop on the edge of the beach, the 'Bonus Kiosk', where they'd brought groceries and the calendar from yesterday.

Sam reached for his wallet.

Ralph took the bundle of notes proffered and stuffed them into the front of his rucksack.

"Isn't it gorgeous here?" said Sam, reaching out to his husband, searching for affection. "You know, it's our wedding anniversary next month? Fourteen years. Ivory."

"Really? Ralph replied, missing the prompt to wrap his arms around Sam, kiss him on the lips, tell him he loved him. Instead, he watched, stone-faced, as tears collected in the corner of his partner's eyes before reaching into his bag to retrieve a warm sandwich.

"Speaking of months, I'm going to take that calendar back. Now. Said she was open twenty-four seven, three sixty-five. Three ninety-six more like. Joker. What a rip-off merchant."

He stomped off through the blistering heat as Sam sloped against a palm tree and stared out to sea.

***

59

"Yes?"

The same old woman who had served them the day before stood behind the counter, hawking like a dumpy vulture over Ralph from the moment he entered. Yesterday, Sam had said he'd found the shopkeeper familiar. Ralph had said that was ridiculous as they were seven thousand kilometres from home and on a desolate beach. Ralph had found her glare vexing.

The door of the 'Bonus Kiosk' swung shut behind him as he trudged up to the counter, trapping him inside with the stifling air. It seemed less well stocked than it had yesterday. The area where the groceries had been stacked was now bare, all save a few two-litre bottles of water, and the exposed wall behind where the produce had been was now sloppily plastered with pages of text. Several hundred loose sheets, ripped from books and pasted willy-nilly as wallpaper.

He looked at where they'd collected eggs, tomatoes and bread from the day before and tried to make sense of the strange scripts covering the wall.

"Hi. I came in yesterday," he said, slapping the calendar down on the counter. "You sold me this. From there." Ralph pressed his angry finger down hard on the disappointing calendar and then thrust the same stiff finger at the rotating display in the centre of the floor, which carried over a hundred more such pieces.

"Ah yes, half price. Bargain," the shopkeeper said, peering at him, over half-moon glasses, through beetle-black eyes.

"I want my money back."

"Sorry. No refunds," she said, thwacking a long length of bamboo cane against a section of pasted text stuck on the wall to their side, where the fruit and veg had been. "Says so here, in the rules."

"Don't be absurd. It's clearly faulty."

"Rules are rules. And here's another," she said, the tip of her stick leading his eyes to another sentence strewn amongst the wall of text: "*Proprietor is always right*."

He leaned in, rubbing the sting of sweat and sun block from his eyes and took a closer look, only to confirm the lady's words.

"This is ludicrous. If an object's faulty, I'm entitled to a refund—it's the law."

"Where you are from, maybe—but you're not home now, are you?" she said and winked and laughed, hee-haw cawing like a randy magpie.

She pushed the calendar back towards him and his eyes were drawn to her hands. Despite the heat, both were gloved in elbow-high black velvet and each gloved finger was decorated with a ring—all except for the fourth finger on her left. Each of the rings bore mounted on it a miniature black bone. Ralph stared at her peculiar attire and felt a shot of ice run down his spine which was anything but refreshing, despite the shop being hotter than an oven. He backed away from the counter and knocked into the carousel which held hundreds of sealed, reduced, identical wall calendars. He managing to grab it to steady it and saved it from tipping over.

His heart revved. How dare this crone speak to him this way, with her stick and her ugly jewellery and her rip-off products and her stupid wall of rules—he wanted his pesos back.

"But it's got an extra month in it. Thirty-one days that don't exist. And after that, the days are all out of whack. It's useless."

"You mean Beachtember."

"Yes, I mean 'Beachtember'. Of course I mean Beachtember," he said, his cheeks firing red. He snatched the calendar up, riffled through its pages and shook the made-up month in the shopkeeper's face.

"Pinch punch first of the month," she said.

"What?"

"First of Beachtember. Today," she said, her thin lips pinned up a little higher on her weathered cheeks, almost breaking into a smile. "Pinch punch."

"You're crazy," he said, pulling out his mobile phone—still with no bars—and tapped on the calendar app to try and prove her wrong. To his shock, when he opened up the calendar widget and displayed it on the screen, it too presented the entire month of Beachtember. "What the—"

"You like the beach? Beautiful, isn't it? Hot white sands, deep blue seas. So peaceful—and all yours. For the entire month."

Ralph switched his phone off and on and off and on, hoping to fix the glitch, but each time, Beachtember flicked back up on the screen.

"I just want my money back," he said, giving up on the phone and sliding it back into the pocket of his trunks.

"No refunds," she said, again tapping her stick against the wall rules, then, swinging her stick towards the carousel, "Happy to exchange for a different calendar."

"What? Do they all have Beachtember in them? I bet they're all the same."

"Yes. Of course. It's Beachtember. Do you want to make a bet?"

"No. No. I don't. No bets. Of course I don't want another one. Look," he said, taking his towel out from his bag and patting the sweat from his face, "What's this all about? Where are the cameras? Joke's over. I get it. I'm being pranked."

"Not at all—no cameras here. No electricity," she said and he realised she spoke the truth. His crazed eyes spun the shop floor. There were no plug sockets in any of the walls, no till, no ceiling lights.

He laughed, feeling his sanity start to melt a little with the heat.

"Tell me about this Beachtember then," he said, exhaling slowly, leaning over and placing both hands on the counter, bringing his face up close to the old hag's.

"Simple. You get to stay on the beach for an entire month. Thirty-one days. Holiday time."

"Sounds great," he said, hot, bothered, with no option but to go along with the woman's game. "Keep your bloody calendar. I'll just take this water. Do you have any crisps?" He pulled a note out from his stash.

"No, we don't sell food. Only food is Bonus Ice Cream. Van comes every Tuesday. Range of flavours. Bound to find one you like. Why not try them all?"

"You were stacked with food yesterday. We brought a bag of groceries!" He gestured at the bare wall to his left, the wall now covered in text. He noticed sand was starting to pour in through a narrow slit at the top, a trickle at first and then, the longer he looked, the faster it came. A gentle, continuous gush cascaded down over the glued book pages and formed a pile where the broccoli had sat the day before.

"No. We've never sold food here. It's in the rules, look." She pointed her bamboo cane at a tiny sentence amongst a page stuck down amongst the wall of other pages. "*No food is sold in this shop.*"

"You're completely mad," he said. "Keep the change." Picking up his water and storming out, he slammed the door behind him.

"What about your free seventeen percent?" she said softly to his back, waving a smaller bottle of water she'd lifted up from behind the counter, but it was too late, he'd gone. "Always something extra with every purchase in the Bonus Kiosk."

***

The sun was strong. Ralph made his way back over to the cluster of trees to find Sam gone. He looked up and down the beach. His husband was nowhere to be seen. Nothing except for blank white sheets of sand in either direction, dense thicket behind, the kiosk and the ocean were in his sight.

"Christ's sake" he said and started to walk back along the beach.

He kept plodding, feet slapping on hot sand, thwump, thwump, thwump, as he searched for the clearing where the path began that would take him back to their rental property.

But he couldn't find it.

On and on along the scorching sand he walked, against the wall of thick jungle to no avail. He tried his phone, its battery draining of juice fast—it still told him it was Beachtember the first, it was still out of service. After walking straight for hours, he'd finished his water and the rest of his salty sandwich. His stomach rumbled and his throat felt dry as the sands.

Ralph could no longer see the kiosk behind him, or the shady bunch of trees, or any shade at all, but still he had not found the path clearing. He contemplated turning around and retracing his steps, but, with his innate bull-headed arrogance, he knew his eyes had not missed the break in the dense shrubbery. And so he continued.

His skin was hot to touch and now a shade of lobster. The sun had taken its full arc of the sky and was touching base on top of the ocean. Mosquitoes chipped at the back of his neck and legs as his feet slapped down and down again, onward.

Then he stopped.

Was he so tired, so dehydrated, so sunburned that he was delusional? He squint to dull the white

65

light of the sun and there, in front of him where it should have been behind, stood the Bonus Kiosk.

n any better state, it would have taken an army of stallions to drag him back into that bastard shop, but as night time was falling fast as it does so close to the equator and as he was out of food and water, he felt he had no other choice but to step back inside to ask for directions.

***

"Yes?"

"Hi," he said, his feet noticing the floor of the shop was now filled with a few inches of sand, his ears hearing the waterfall of sand tipping in hard and fast from the hole in the wall. "Look, I—"

"Came back for your bonus water?"

His red face twinged with pain as it became screwed up with confusion.

The lady plonked down a small bottle of water on the counter top.

"No, but... well, yes. Thanks," he said, swiping the bottle, unscrewing it with haste and gulping the liquid down. "I'd like to buy another. Please. Two." He slammed down a note on the counter.

"About earlier... sorry. Too much of this darn sun." A smile forced its way onto just his lips.

"We all have our mad moments," she said.

"Could you just direct me back to the path, back to the rentals?"

"Path? No paths in Beachtember. Just sand, sea, sun. And ice cream on a Tuesday."

"Pardon?"

"No paths. You're on the beach. I told you. Pinch punch. It's Beachtember. Thirty-one days."

"You're saying I'm trapped on the beach?"

"Well, yes."

"As in, stuck here. Can't leave. For a month?"

"Yes. It's beautiful isn't it? Postcard picture perfect. Like to buy a postcard?" She gestured at a range of cards, each one a variation on a theme, each one an image of the hot ball of fire in the sky touching down on the top of the ocean, each one radiating more unwanted heat at Ralph.

"No. No thanks," he paused, considering his manners—this was the only shop they'd spotted for miles when they'd arrived at their destination yesterday. He needed to be polite. "But I've no food."

"Ice cream," she winked. "Bonus Kiosk does ice cream. Every Tuesday."

"It's Monday."

"Yes. Monday the first of Beachtember. Ice cream tomorrow. Ice cream on a Tuesday. So many flavours."

"But it's getting dark outside. What am I supposed to do? Where do I sleep?" His legs ached like he'd run a marathon, his feet were sore and the sun had burned not only his exposed skin, but the skin that had been hidden under his t-shirt and shorts.

"We sell hammocks. Come with a free bottle of mosquito spray," she said. "Bonus Kiosk—always a bonus with every purchase." She pointed at the few pieces of stock, pushed up against the wall that was not covered in writing, mostly still in brown cardboard boxes.

"I guess I'll take a hammock and some spray then," Ralph said, pulling out another note. His brain needed rest and his body needed some kind of miracle. Over half the money Sam had given him he'd spent in this woman's kiosk already.

He left the shop without saying thank you or goodbye, set his hammock up under the trees and lay in it under only the light of a full moon and the flickering night sign above the Kiosk's door. As night came, Ralph, suffering from severe exposure, struggled to distinguish the stars in the sky from imagined stars that flickered in and out of what remained of his peripheral vision. Moments of pained, restless, fretful sleep ensued.

***

Ralph woke at the crack of dawn from fitful sleep and found himself scratching—the mosquito spray hadn't worked. Ralph glugged down a few mouthfuls of water, each mouthful feeling like deep-throating cacti. The night had not been good.

His phone told him it was five o'clock in the morning, the second of Beachtember. He was still there, imprisoned on the beach and his skin was blistered, red, nibbled and sore. He rubbed the sleep from his eyes and fantasised about coffee and eggs and paracetamol as he took another sip from the bottle. He'd have to drink more slowly if he was going to be here for the month, he thought. He itched his forearms and shins and strips of skin like fried bacon sheared off under his nails.

He rocked himself with care out of his hammock and slid his flip flops on, snapping the thong on one as he did.

"Shit. Shit shit shit shit shit," he said, lobbing the broken footwear into the thicket behind him. He couldn't do another night on this beach let alone another twenty-nine days. The sun was already churning out its fire. He looked out to the horizon, blurred by the haze of morning and sun-singed retina and placed his bare foot down on the sand in the shade.

Tolerable. Just.

If he was going to walk the other direction in order to escape he knew he needed to do it now, before the sun rose any higher and turned the sand into lava, into burning coals. He packed his stuff up and set off in the other direction.

He'd been walking for several hours, nothing but undrinkable water and bramble to his right and to his left, and white sand underfoot, when he saw a red shape on the shore in the distance. He mustered his inner strength and ran toward the red shape, which turned out to be a tent.

"Digs," he shouted into the void around him. Never before in his life had the thought of something so dull as dusting off dirt from very old things dug up from beneath the ground made him so happy. There must be people there who could direct him. He thought briefly of Sam. Maybe he'd be there, inside, exploring whatever old fossils had been excavated. *Bloody ammonites*, he cussed aloud.

He lifted up the canvas curtain of the tent, dipped his head and entered. It was muggier inside than out, at least the canvas roof offered protection from the deadly rays. The tent was more than empty. Where the sand should have been was a pit, propped open with wooden struts/ Its edge was scattered with abandoned spades and brushes. Ralph edged closer and saw at the bottom of the pit what looked like a row of black elephant tusks poking up and out of the sand, a linear bunch of sharp-nailed fingers. It didn't look like fossils, more like bones. If bones were black and serrated.

The bones seemed to beckon him closer, offering whispers of refreshment and direction.

He climbed down the sandy walls of the pit and neared the bottom. He reached out, enticed by a beseeching murmur that seemed to speak to his heart coming from within the pit. He placed his hand on a black bony finger poking up through the sands. It brought an instant coldness to his fingertips, causing him to lose balance and topple over. A sheet of sand slid down, burying the black finger tips. Or had they sunk of their own accord? He rubbed his eyes with sandy hands, jumped up and back, unsure of what he'd just seen.

The walls of the tent suddenly felt a little closer, as if closing in. And Ralph wanted out.

He climbed up out of the pit and floundered out of the tent. He looked ahead to the journey he had no choice but to continue. But where before had been nothing but more white sand, now he could see the kiosk again. He'd clearly come full circle.

Exhaustion and frustration shook hands with pain and despair as the sun beat down on his red raw face.

The fire of the sand burned through his bare foot, ricocheting pain up his leg. Layers of skin on his sole became hot, the acrid stench of his own flesh cooking slapped him in the nose. He hopped on his flip-flopped foot and hurried down to the edge of the sea. He dipped his feet, howling with pain as the salt of the water bit like lemon sharks. He held and looked at his foot which had been cauterised by the griddle of the sand. It had cooled slightly under the surface of the water and he saw his foot had lost its toes.

His heart thrummed like a bag of bees. There was no way left or right to escape, the beach was an infinite loop. He'd need a machete to get through the greenery at the top of the shore and would most likely only be returned to the spot from which he had begun. His only option was to swim. *Away from this bastard place.*

He bundled his belongings into his bag which he balanced on top of his head and waded out into the water, salt stinging every inch of his flesh, infiltrating open wounds with toxic marine bacteria.

It got so deep that he had no choice but to swim and he did as far as he could. Tendrils of seaweed and unknown creatures tangled and snagged against his legs in the dark waters.

He felt exhausted, his body was sick, close to collapsing and dropping like a rock to the ocean floor and his mind skirted dangerously close to cracking. Pain pin-balled through every part of him.

Just as he thought he could swim no more, game over, his foot hit the sea bed. Both feet. He put his raw soles flat on the rough terrain below the water which he still could not see clearly he began to walk again. Sharp shells, rocks, needles, teeth of glass: for all he knew this lay along the ocean carpet. Razor clams or razor blades took off more flesh from his feet and legs. His shins and thighs, rended by things of the deep, puffed swirls of smoke-like red out into the water behind him.

The sun hung directly above and his shoulders, exposed again as the water became shallow, bubbled with pearly blisters. In front of him, a strip of white grew taller until it became the sands of a beach like the shoreline he had swum from.

And it *was* the shore line he had swum away from. There in front where it should have been behind stood the cluster of trees and the Bonus Kiosk.

***

Ralph got out of the water and shipwrecked himself under the collection of palms. Sand stuck in his countless wounds, decorating his body like salted tiger stripes. He looked like he'd been peeled. Badly. He passed out.

***

Hours or days later, Ralph was woken by music. The minor key of 'Greensleeves' caromed through the thick air into his ears. He fumbled in his bag, found a bottle and drained it of its last few drops of water. His eyes, fried like egg albumen, made out the silhouette of a truck in the distance. Tuesday. *Must be Tuesday,* he thought, remembering the shopkeeper's words. Ice cream Tuesday. He watched the truck progress toward him until it pulled up at his pitch.

He pulled out a note from his bag and stumbled toward it, the sand a little cooler, more tolerable in the evening light.

"Yes?" said the lady, the same shopkeeper from the kiosk, as she picked up a scooper.

"Ice cream," he murmured, his words barely forming.

"Flavour?" she asked reaching around and pointing with her cane at the options displayed on the side of her truck.

"Can't read. My eyes," he said, each black pupil hidden behind white fog.

"Ah, solar cataracts."

"Don't care what flavour. Anything. Need to eat."

"Okay. Well, today, we have special flavours for our special customer to celebrate the first of Beachtember. We have: 'Can't Believe It's Not Chicken', 'Tallow 'n' Shavings' or 'Miscellaneous'."

He felt a dry wretch of vomit burning up his throat. Still the first? Surely not. And this wasn't ice cream. But it wasn't July and this wasn't a holiday.

73

"Miscellaneous. Please," he croaked, desperate.

"Here you go. Complimentary flake," she said, snapping off her un-ringed finger, sucking out the marrow and shoving it on the top of the cream ball in its cone. She dressed the cold treat with a squeeze of strawberry sauce from her stump. Ralph largely sunblind, was oblivious to it all. "Bonus ice cream."

Ralph bit into it with fervour only to spit it back onto the floor of the beach.

"That's fucking disgusting," he said, dropping the cone, followed by buckled waves of dry-heaving.

He stood up, wiping his face with his hand, lumps of minced, frozen cartilaginous gunk sloughing off from his cheeks onto the floor. Ralph was unsure if the textured slush was ice cream or parts of his face, but hurled again as he caught the scent of his fingertips which stank of the dankest fetid rot.

"Maybe. But it's all you're getting," she said slamming the shutter down and driving off, leaving a trail of melody, 'You Are My Sunshine,' hanging behind in the air so heavy you could cut it with a knife.

"And you didn't give me my change," he shouted whilst shuffling back across the beach, a ribbon of bodily detritus behind him.

Back at the shady patch under the trees, he curled his aching body up in the hammock. A soft whoop from above stilled his breath. Through opaque eyes, he picked out large wings circling. And then more—could it be a wake of vultures bothering the blue sky? A black beast of feathers cut through the air, dive-bombing down towards him. In one fell swoop, the bird of prey clean tore off the hand that still stank of vomit and meat cone and flew off with it in its talons.

Ralph screamed in agony. Blood squirted from the end of his arm, making a ruddy mess of the sand. He pulled his towel from his bag and wrapped it around and around his wrist stump, then folded over in pain in the hammock, screaming and crying all the while. Ralph knew he would die if he didn't do something, if he didn't try to leave the bay.

His only option was to go back in the kiosk.

With his last modicum of strength, he dragged himself up and out of the hammock, placed one painful foot in front of the other and got underway. He'd had enough. He was going to demand she helped him. *Or God help her*, he thought.

He forced the door open, stepped into the shop, left hand raw, right hand gone, bandaged in a crimson towel. He staggered to the counter in search of the lady. Every step through the rising sands of the shop floor hurt. Sand was flooding in through the gap in the wall, faster and thicker than on his last visit.

"Yes?" Same greeting, same beady eyes, same fists full of black rings.

Without words, he pulled out the last remaining notes from his bag. Then with the only word his dehydrated lips could muster: "Help."

He ushed the last of his money over the counter and, with his left hand, he gathered two bottles of water from the shelf.

"Bonus water," she said, swiftly shoving the notes amongst her cleavage, and placing two additional, miniature bottles on the counter. "Everything you buy comes with added bonus. Bonus Kiosk."

She placed a coin of change on the counter and pushed it toward him. After downing half a bottle, he managed to regain a reedy voice. "Thanks," his rasped.

"Your change," she said.

He looked at the coin. It wasn't enough for more water. "Keep it," he said. "S'not worth anything to me. S'not enough for water. Still no food in?"

She lifted her stick and pointed it towards the wall of writing. "We don't sell—"

"Yeah. I get it. Rules. Don't sell food."

"Correct—but if you want something in exchange for your coin, I could offer you some entertainment..." Her voice trailed off as she shuffled out from the counter, past the calendar carousel and over to a shelf.

"What do I want with bloody entertainment? Look at the state of me. I need urgent medical attention. I'm burnt—no toes, no hand. I've a fever too, infected. I'll die if you don't help me," he said. Odorous pus seeped from wet wounds from countless sites on his body. "Look at my legs. A butcher's bin."

"Looks like lumpy ice cream," she said, licking her lips.

"And my eyes. I can't see further than the ends of my hands. Hand! Something took my right hand, for Christ's sake. Help me, you witch!"

"We've entertainment," she said. "It's only the first of Beachtember. Entertainment might help you pass time quicker."

He let out a crazed laugh. "Pass time quicker? Without water, food, antibiotics, a bloody good surgeon... I'm going to die!"

She reached down, picked up a small packet from the shelf and carried it to the counter. "Cards," she said. Ralph recognised the rectangular packet, the black and white lattice pattern of the box immediately. "You can afford these."

Ralph sighed. He brought his spread hand up to his forehead and shook his head into it in despair, his eyes winced with pain as his hand made contact with the raw, cracked, oozing, infected skin of his brow.

"Play me and win," the crone said, her black eyes narrowing, "and I'll help you home."

He dropped his hand and looked up. "For real? All I've got to do is beat you at cards and you'll get me out of this shit hole? This... zero star holiday trashcan?"

"Yes. Name your game."

"Now you're talking," he said, dragging a small step ladder through the rising sand of the shop floor to perch on, with little strength left for standing. "What have I got to lose?"

"Exactly," the lady said, with a sparkle of ruby to her eye.

"Poker," Ralph said, his eyes also brightening, despite his weathered body burning and shedding and flaking layers of purulent skin with every movement he made, unwrapping with every heartbeat.

"Let's play a few games for fun first, to warm up," she said, brushing black feathers from the counter and placing down the cards.

"Sure," he said. He took a swig on his water. "I used to be pretty good at this though, I'll warn you early doors."

***

Time unlike no other passed as his exhaustion and fever grew, his pain ebbed and ebbed. His hand throbbed and dripped onto the rising sands, but being the addict he was, he got a buzz from the cards. The buzz spurred him onward. Each win seemed to energize him, to power him on. Bursts of adrenaline and dopamine got him through each round.

The lady played poorly, despite her face as old and still as the fossils the beach held and Ralph started to feel a minutiae of hope. Addiction demons roared inside his gnarled, empty guts, with each win, he felt a little closer to home.

"Let's do it. One final hand. I'm ready. I need you to take me to Sam, to hospital." A pool of blood had collected around him, a circle of flies hovered over his stump. The sand in the shop had risen up to his knees.

"Final game then," the lady said, palming out fresh cards. "This is it."

He lifted his hand, drew his pair close to his face to check what he thought he could just about see. Through his near-opaque eyes, Ralph saw the one-eyed suicide king winking at him, axe in hand and the Jack, the laughing boy—a diamond too. On the counter top lay an old queen, diamond and the ten too amongst the row of shared cards. The game played on, his hopes of rescue elevated. The shopkeeper twisted over the final card on the countertop, ace of diamonds and Ralph yelled out from his seat, "Fuck yeah. I'm going home!"

Royal flush. An unbeatable hand. *Unbelievable* he thought and yelled again.

He slammed his fist down on the counter so hard the postcard display fell over. "Yes! All in. Get the fuck in! Yes yes yes yes yes. Thank the fucking Lord. You won't beat this. You can't beat this," he said.

He spread his cards out wide so the old lady could see his luck, his heart banged as he waited with bated breath for her to reveal hers. Sand poured in, waist height. "Hurry up, you old hag. Get me out of here."

She tilted her head to one side and looked at the state of a man in front of her.

"I've won, haven't I? That's it. I can go home," he shouted, white spittle frothing like lace at the corners of his mouth.

"I'm sorry," she said stepping back from the counter and tossing her hand down for him to see.

He looked down at her cards and up at the lady and down at the cards again.

"What is this> What is this one here? This card? With the bowl on it. Here," He tapped the odd card with his finger, his red face becoming white. Where a Jack or Queen or King normally would be found, on this picture card, was an image of what appeared to be a bowl or a cauldron with a handle.

"I'm afraid you have lost," she said, picking up the card, and tipping it forwards towards the countertop. "As I have the Bucket of Skulls."

Hundreds of small, bir-like and humanoid skulls, ebony black, spilled out from the bucket on the card like rice from a bag. All over the counter, out and onto the floor skulls tumbled, spreading out as they came thick and fast with and into the sand that was ever rising in the beach shop.

Ralph, a face full of panic, looked up at the woman and brushed the flood of skulls away from where he was getting stuck. "No, this can't be. There's no such card!"

She lifted her stick and tapped it up high on the wall of words behind him where the fruit and vegetables used to be. "*Bucket of Skulls wins outright*," she said with a squawk in her voice.

Ralph scrabbled together all of the cards, including the rogue one from the Bucket suit, which was still hurling out small skulls and counted them three times: fifty-three, fifty-three, fifty-three.

"There's an extra card, you can't do that, you can't bring in new suits," he wailed.

"Bonus card," she said, and then tapped the rules on the wall again. "Bucket of Skulls *always* wins. Beachtember always wins."

Even with his poor eyes, he could see her neck elongating, coming up out of the white ruff of her black dress. Her hair fell out and black feathers spurted through the puckered skin of her head in replacement. Two nubs burst out from her clavicle and branched wide and sideways, each pronged with more feathers, longer, darker, sharpened at their tips like blades. Her mouth pinched forwards, grew forwards, and reddened and became beaklike.

A surge of vomit and anger rose up into his throat. Ralph was scared. Ralph was angry—angry at the lady beyond belief, angry at his own eyes for failing him in such an evil way. He yelled, "I'm going to kill you, you crazy old bitch!"

He dragged himself out of the sand and, despite his stump, he lunged over toward the counter to try and grab the woman by her shoulders. He wanted to shake her hard like he shook Sam. He needed to beat sense into the vitriolic old crone like he had beaten his husband so many times before, but his arms—instead of meeting the now aquiline hag to crush her, came crashing in together. Shockwaves of pain sped through his burned and bitten torso as his hand and stump collided. Ralph fell forward in agony.

The woman had gone, vanished, leaving just Ralph in the shop, now up to his chest in sand. Only her caw of a voice remained. It left a final sentence pegged to the thick air of the shop with laughter: "Bonus life for me. You can't kill the un-dead." The

81

words pecked at his ear drums, as if driving glass shards into his brain. He needed to get out of the kiosk, away from her hellish nest of sand and cards and faulty calendars.

A panic to end all states of panic washed over Ralph's very quiddity. He scooped his way out pell-mell, as fast as the sand would allow and managed to get away from the kiosk of the bird-witch and back into the heat of the beach.

Had he lost the plot completely? He staggered until he was as far away from the Bonus Kiosk as he could possibly manage, each slap of foot on sand burning like murder, sending lightning bolts of agony jolting through his body.

He was screaming and burning, exposed to the heat of the sun and the sand again and

could go no further. He dropped to his knees as the red tent appeared again before him.

He crawled through canvas wings and found himself back in the pit where the black finger-bones had lain.

Sand gave way beneath his weak wrist and feet and he rolled down into the pit, the sides of which caved in after. The excavation site had been dug deeper, revealing not black fingers, nor tusks poking up from the beach floor, but a ribcage, black and bone, belonging to an entirely black skeleton. The skeleton was cold to the touch as his cheek slammed into it. It felt hard and smooth against his damaged torso, as if made from ivory. Like whittle-sharp elephant tusks, the finger-like projections skewered his core, leaving his broken, bleeding body hung like a sandy, rotten kebab. Ralph hung from the bones of his own black ribcage. In unison, one guttural moan came from Ralph and one from the bones on the beach as Ralph closed his eyes for the last time and his soul sank down into a sandy, flaming hot vortex.

The roof of the red tent flew off, carried up into the air and away, by a ruby-eyed vulture, leaving Ralph's body to barbecue alone in the sun.

***

The following morning, August 1st, Sam woke up in tears as his husband had still not returned. He ran down to the beach. In the light of the day, he could see the white sands and the ocean that appeared to stretch out eternally in all directions. At the furthest point his wet eyes could resolve, out far on the white hot sands, Sam saw something black, like the prongs of a fork, like black fingers, or the bones of a ribcage poking up from the beach.

He ran towards what he thought could only be a mirage, but as he got closer, he realised it wasn't. He fell down on his knees, hands covering his mouth, as he arrived at the body of his husband. Ralph lay there, splayed in the sand, pecked at, torn like teased ham.

He knelt down by Ralph's side and reached for the left hand of his dead lover to take it in his own. Where Ralph's wedding ring once was, the ugly ring Ralph's aunt had bequeathed him squeezed dead flesh and bone.

***

And in the Bonus Kiosk which looked out over the beach, a newcomer was selecting groceries from the well-stocked shelves and browsing plentiful souvenirs to send his family back home. He asked the shopkeeper, whom he thought resembled a fat vulture, if she had anything cheap he could purchase as a gift for the chore that were his children.

"We have nothing really in here for children, Sir, I'm afraid... perhaps I could interest you in a small gift for yourself? How about a little something to decorate your holiday let with—to bring a little sunshine to the walls." She shuffled to the central carousel. "Perhaps you'd be interested in one of our half-price calendars,,,"

Blood Worms

Jason R Frei

A storm raged outside the derelict warehouse. The bruised blue-black night sky lit up like a telephone switchboard as lightning flashed across its expanse.

Fog rolled in as rotten as corpses in a graveyard. Rain froze as the temperature quickly dropped. The wind kicked up and ripped through the alleys, upending trash cans and sending debris flying through the air.

A strange muttering sounded on the wind, like the whispering of the dead and dying. The misty fog roiled and surged like a witch's cauldron. Lightning struck the roof of the warehouse, tearing a hole through it. The baying on the wind grew shriller like the whistle of a freight train.

Inside the warehouse, dust and garbage blew around in miniature cyclones. Tattered cobwebs danced across the walls and floor. Pieces of glass skittered across the floor like spiders on a pond. Lying in the center of the cracked cement floor was a man. His ebony skin shimmered in greenish-gray light.

The fog entered the warehouse. A scuttling sound from inside the shadowy cloud rose above the shrieking on the wind. Another bolt of lightning cascaded through the opening in the roof, hit the floor and sent concrete into the air like shrapnel. It coursed through the body, causing it to dance and shake. Smoke rose from the man's bald head and his trimmed goatee smoldered. The flailing of the body shook a ring from his left hand. It rolled in a tight circle before disappearing into a crack in the floor.

The lightning ran its course and the body stopped shaking. The wind and rain ceased. The night quieted. The moon peeked out from under the clouds. An inaudible sigh escaped from the man's lips and chased the fog away.

He sat up slowly, his brown eyes shining like those of an animal as he surveyed the room.

"Where…?" His voice cracked.

The empty room did not have the answer he looked for. He stood up and, unbeknownst to him, his wallet fell to the floor and opened. The driver's license read "Anthony Walker". Anthony shuffled out into the night.

Moments later, a wet sound issued from inside a crack in the cement. Several tendrils reached over the edge of the hole. They attached themselves to the ground and up heaved a writhing mass of worms the color of blood. The thickest of the worms was as fat as a thumb. The mass squelched and squirmed as it followed Anthony's footsteps.

***

Anthony wandered aimlessly, looking for anything that would jog his memory. He stopped in front of a storefront and caught his own reflection in

86

the glass. He stared hard at the man looking back, but there was no glimmer of recognition.

He turned down an alley, lost in his own thoughts, when a mugger stepped out of the shadows, holding a knife.

"Gimme your wallet," said the thief, "and you won't get hurt."

Anthony turned to run and felt a thump between his shoulder blades. He pivoted and grabbed the assailant's arm. The man's eyes bulged and his mouth formed an O. Anthony twisted the arm, dislocating it with a sickening crunch. The man howled and dropped to his knees. Anthony drove his fist down into the man's face. Blood spurted upwards like a geyser. A wet gurgling sound escaped from the would-be mugger's shattered mouth. Anthony brought his knee up into his chin, knocking him cold.

Before Anthony could catch his breath, a gunshot echoed from the mouth of the alley. Anthony dove to the ground. He rolled to cover and felt pressure between his shoulder blades. He reached around and pulled a knife out of his back.

Anthony stood up and took a shotgun blast point blank to his chest, driving him backwards into a dumpster. He bounced off and lunged at the man with the shotgun. He went in low and drove the knife straight up into the man's stomach and twisted. Blood gushed over his hand. He let go of the knife and swept the man's feet out from under him. He heard sirens in the distance and ran off down the alley as if the devil himself was giving chase.

Anthony ran until the city no longer boxed him in. He found himself on a tree-lined street with houses that all followed the same design. He selected one that looked empty and forced open the front door.

He went upstairs to the bathroom and looked at himself in the mirror. The shotgun blast had torn his shirt to shreds. Oddly enough, no blood stained the clothes or his flesh and he felt no pain. He stripped off his clothes, looked himself over in the mirror and noticed there were no marks from the scuffle in the alley. He felt no pain, no heat, no cold--nothing.

He shook his head and went into the adjoining bedroom. There he opened the top drawer of the dresser. Inside was a set of car keys, a roll of twenty dollar bills and a gun with two full clips. The rest of the drawers were full of clothes.

He quickly got dressed. He balled up his old clothes to throw them away, but first checked the pockets and found a receipt for Gus's Gas. The address and phone number were printed neatly at the top. Finally, his first real clue.

He started back down the stairs, but stopped halfway. A noise near the bottom caught his attention. He peered into the darkness, but saw nothing.

Two steps from the bottom, he stepped in something that squished, like a greasy pile of rotting garbage. He pulled a lighter from his pocket and flicked the flame on.

He stood in a writing pile of thick worms. There were objects mixed among the worms, swirling like garbage in a storm drain. One ring in particular looked familiar, but was then lost as the heap shifted. A worm snaked its way up his leg and thrust itself into his flesh. Anthony screamed out in pain. The worm burrowed halfway into his calf. He grabbed the end of the worm and pulled it out, shaking and swearing down the street. The mass of worms slowly followed.

***

Gus's Gas looked like every other small gas station across America. The kind of place that people passing through would stop, fill up their tanks and bellies and keep moving right along without a second thought.

The young boy attending the front counter had a pimply face, oily hair and the bored eyes of someone trapped in a dead end life. He put down his magazine when Anthony walked in, looked up and cracked a huge grin.

"Hey, man. Glad you're back. You left your stuff here the other night."

He rummaged under the counter and then put a pack of cigarettes, two candy bars, a bottle of soda and a pregnancy test on the top.

Anthony scratched his head and gave the kid an embarrassed look. "Do you remember what night that was? I was hammered."

The kid grinned. "It was just last night."

"Do you remember where I went after?"

89

"Nah, man. You ran outta here calling for your girl."

"My girl?"

"Yeah. A white girl. Short blond hair and a tight red dress. You called her Honey." The kid continued, "You guys took off pretty quick."

"Can you remember anything else?" asked Anthony.

The kid shook his head and then his eyes lit up. "You know, now that you mention it, some dude came in right after."

"Some dude?"

"White guy with a blond buzz cut and a scar down the side of his face. Looked like one of them neo-Nazis that used to run through here. He asked if I knew you--but I didn't tell him anything."

Anthony thanked the kid, gave him a twenty, put the items in his pocket and left.

"Dammit," he thought. "Why can't I remember anything?"

He opened the cigarettes, shook one out and lit it, inhaling deeply. He exhaled the smoke quickly, like an arrow from his mouth. He looked at the cigarette, confused. In the past, he enjoyed the taste of the smoke as it filled his lungs. This cigarette had no taste. A feeling of dread settled over him. Without hesitating, he stabbed the lit end of the cigarette into the palm of his hand. He felt nothing. He continued to grind the cigarette into his hand. The flesh puckered and a little twist of smoke rose up, but there was no pain. Anthony dropped the cigarette and watched the raw, ragged hole in his hand. In less than a minute, the hole closed up and his charred flesh returned to normal.

"Holy shit," said Anthony to himself. "I'm fuckin' dead."

The thought rocketed through his brain and images formed quickly, like a film on fast forward. He could not comprehend what he was seeing. He screwed his eyes shut and took a few deep breaths, centering himself. The images slowed down.

He saw himself with a woman. They held hands and laughed. They seemed younger, filled with life.

The next image showed the two of them in a Wal-Mart, shoplifting. They laughed and watched only each other.

The scene shifted. They walked through a department store. They snatched more expensive items, like jewelry and electronics. They both still smiled.

Fast forward. Another jewelry store, but this time, the image showed three of them. A white man with short hair and a scar on his cheek joined them. They all laughed. The name Sean flashed across the screen of Anthony's mind.

Fast forward again. Now they hit jewelry stores and used guns, but the smiles and laughs faded. Their mouths turned hard, serious, angry.

Next scene. Anthony and Honey sat alone. They held each other and laughed. Honey held Anthony's hand on her stomach and beamed radiantly. A single tear tracked down Anthony's smiling face.

One last scene. Anthony and Sean argued. They wrestled over a gun. There was a bang and a scream.

Anthony fell to his knees, retching. Nothing came up, but he could not stop. Over and over, his stomach lurched and his throat dilated. His eyes bulged in his head, but no tears fell. When he felt that he could take no more, the assault on his body ceased.

***

Anthony remembered everything. He met Honey when he was just seventeen. He sat on the hood of his car outside the high school, smoking a cigarette, when he first saw her. Men surrounded her, even then. He just watched as she walked closer. His eyes never left her, memorized every aspect of her, her body, her smile, the way she walked, the way the sun blazed on her blonde hair, the way her dress hugged just the right parts. He caught her eye, nodded and smiled. She smiled right back, tossed her hair and walked up to him. The other men took defensive positions, like linebackers protecting their quarterback.

"Hello," she said, her voice rimmed with sugar. "I'm Honey."

"You sure are," said Anthony. A smile played across his lips.

Honey turned to her entourage and dismissed them in a way that made them think it was their idea. "Thanks for walking me over here, boys. I think I've got this on my own now."

She blew them a kiss and waved goodbye. They took turns looking back and eyeing up Anthony as they walked away.

Anthony snorted.

"You sure do have a way with the boys," he said.

"Boys are easy," she said as she took a seat next to him on the hood. "A smile and a little wiggle and they do whatever I want."

"Maybe those kinds of boys," replied Anthony.

"Oh, and what kind of boy are you?" teased Honey.

"Oh, I'm no boy, Honey. I'm a man."

"Is that so? What makes you a man and them, boys?"

"I've got plans. Big plans. I'm gonna be someone, and it won't be because someone gave it to me. I'm going to take what I deserve. That's what makes me a man."

"So, men take what they want, is that it? And are you going to take me then, you big man?"

Anthony jumped down and turned into her before she could say anything else. He put one arm around her back, the other cupped her head and he kissed her full on her ruby red lips. Her eyes grew wide and she stiffened, but only for a moment. Then she grabbed him and pulled him closer, her tongue exploring his.

They spent the rest of their year inseparable. They were wild and crazy kids and they completely loved each other.

Neither one of them grew up in a good home, so they moved into a small apartment together.

Anthony got a part-time job working on cars and Honey cleaned rooms at a hotel. They stole food first out of necessity, but then it just became fun. It was like a game--who could steal the most.

Soon enough, they found they could steal things that were worth money. They lifted jewelry and watches from the counters at local stores. They made it look easy and they loved each other more and more every day.

All good things must come to an end and so it was for Anthony and Honey. They got caught shoplifting at a Macys. Instead of calling the police, the guard made them a deal. He wanted the three of them to go into business together, robbing jewelry stores. He saw the way they worked together and knew it would work. He had connections to fence the jewelry and supply them with guns. They agreed and that was how they met Sean.

At first it was fun. They would hit small stores and no one got hurt. Sean stood guard as Honey and Anthony cleaned out the counters. They made good money, but Sean wanted more. His plans got more elaborate and the stores got bigger. Sean and Anthony argued after almost every job. It was no longer a game nor was it fun.

Honey and Anthony wanted to be done with the whole business. They told Sean that the next heist would be their last. He fumed and screamed and plotted. He told them that he kept a drawer full of evidence that could send them away forever. Anthony reminded him that the heists were his idea and they would take him down too if he tried

94

anything. Sean seethed, but agreed to one more heist.

After the confrontation, Anthony took Honey home and then ran out to the grocery store. When he got back, Honey sat on the couch. She asked him to sit with her. He put the groceries in the kitchen and then sat on the couch.

"I got you a present," said Honey.

"Oh really?" asked Anthony, smiling. "Did I miss an anniversary?"

"Not yet," said Honey and handed him a small, wrapped box.

With a grin on his face, he tore open the box. Inside was a pregnancy test, with a red plus on it. Anthony gasped and looked up.

"You're pregnant!" He had a grin on his face and his eyes were wide.

"I think so," she said. Her voice wavered. "What do you think?"

Anthony dropped the test and squeezed Honey harder than he ever had before.

"I'm going to be a father," he said.

Honey placed Anthony's hand on her stomach, closed her eyes and smiled.

"Just to be sure, we should get another test," said Honey. "You know these aren't always reliable."

"After dinner, we'll run out," said Anthony. "We should get something to celebrate."

"All I want right now is a candy bar and some ginger ale."

Anthony laughed and held Honey even tighter.

Anthony's mind reeled. The memories flooded him, drowning out everything else. He had to find Honey before it was too late.

Anthony walked back to the city. He snuck into a parking garage and took the stairs to the top floor. He found a car covered in orange parking tickets tucked under the windshield wipers and broke into it. After he dug the wires out from under the dash and stripped the two he needed, he settled back in his seat.

Time to let more memories cone back. He closed his eyes, breathed in deep and opened his mind.

***

After Anthony and Honey had eaten, they drove to the nearest 24 hour convenience store-Gus's Gas. Honey blared the music with the top down as the wind blew her hair out behind her.

When they got to the store, Honey stayed in the car and Anthony ran inside. He grabbed a pregnancy test and a ginger ale. He went up to the counter, stopped and went back to the candy aisle. He got himself a Milky Way and for Honey, a peanut butter Twix. It was her favorite and he would deny her nothing on this night.

Anthony went up to the counter. The kid working the front was definitely not Gus. He was young. He put down the magazine he held in his hands.

"How can I help you?" he asked.

Anthony put his things on the counter.

"Can I get a pack of Camels?" replied Anthony.

The kid took down the Camels and rang everything up. "That'll be $8.35."

Anthony gave the kid a ten and looked out the window. He saw a black Trans Am screech into the lot. Anthony recognized it instantly.

Sean got out of his car and tucked a gun in his front waistband. Without waiting for his change or grabbing his items, Anthony ran out the front door. He yelled for Honey and pointed over at Sean. Anthony made a beeline straight for Sean.

"What the fuck are you doing here?" said Anthony. "Are you following us?"

Sean smirked at Anthony. "Hey now, that's no way to greet a partner. We've got a job tomorrow night."

Anthony started to open his mouth.

"Yeah, yeah, I know," said Sean, rolling his eyes and adding in a sarcastic voice, "Your last job. Whatever, man, just meet at the warehouse tomorrow morning and don't be fucking late."

Anthony stormed off and got in the car with Honey. She slammed it into reverse and gave Sean the finger as she peeled out of the parking lot.

"I can't believe the nerve of him," said Honey. "Who the fuck does he think he is, telling us what to do?"

"Seriously," replied Anthony. "I'll be glad when this shit is over. I can't take his attitude anymore."

Anthony sat up quickly. Something disturbed his memories. He strained to hear what his subconscious warned him of. He settled back in his seat when a fat red tentacle reached up over the hood of the car. A gold ring encircled the worm.

Anthony sparked the stripped wires together and the car roared to life. He turned on the lights and floored it in reverse. The wormy collective bounced to the ground. Anthony slammed the shifter into Drive and sped off. He looked in the rearview mirror. The scattered worms regrouped and started their chase anew.

Anthony went as fast as he could through the parking garage, sliding sideways out onto the adjoining road. He tore through the empty streets until he found an abandoned, weed-covered parking lot. He drove to the back of the lot, turned off the lights and killed the engine.

He got out of the car, shaking and took some deep breaths to calm himself. When the shaking subsided, he got back in the car, checked the rearview mirror for any sign of the worms and then closed his eyes and let the memories continue.

***

Anthony and Honey got up early the next morning and packed their gear. They went to the warehouse, parking the Plymouth inside. Sean had a map and a blueprint laid out on the table. He smiled when they walked in.

"Glad you made it. I almost thought you'd try to run, but you're not that stupid."

"Fuck off, Sean," said Honey. "We said we'd do one more job, so keep your comments to yourself.

"This job should be the last one for all of us," said Sean. "The diamond exchange downtown is holding on to a large supply of loose diamonds for an exhibit at the museum. Hundreds of 'em, worth millions."

Anthony and Honey looked at each other and smiled.

"All right," said Anthony. "What's the plan?"

"It's easy. They're loading up the diamonds tonight. One armored van will be arriving in the back around midnight. They'll have two guards with the van and three more inside the exchange. And I've got this…"

Sean reached into his gear bag and pulled out a smoke grenade. Anthony and Honey's eyes grew wide and their faces lit up.

"Once all the guards are inside, we toss this and go in hot. We grab everything we can and get out in less than sixty seconds. They'll already have everything bagged up for us."

"Ok," said Anthony, nodding his head. "So the grab is easy. What about after?"

"My fence won't be in town for a few days, so Honey, you'll have to use one of your old bank boyfriends and hide the diamonds until my guy gets in."

"Easy peasy," said Honey as she winked at Anthony, "I know just the guy."

"All right," said Sean. "We'll meet here at ten to get everything ready."

Honey and Anthony took a cab back to their apartment and prepared for the evening. They were both in good spirits.

"This is it, babe," said Honey. "No more jobs after this."

"That's right, just the three of us living large," he said, looking at Honey's belly.

She rubbed her hand over her stomach.

"I'm going to get so fat," she laughed.

Anthony grabbed her by the waist, spun her around and kissed her. They were in heaven.

***

The euphoria still rode high when they got to the warehouse that night. Sean looked on in disgust as the couple stopped every five minutes to kiss and grope each other.

"Knock it off," he finally growled. "We've got shit to do and neither one of you are focused. This is the most important job we've done. You need to be sharp."

"Sorry, daddy," said Honey, lowering her eyes as if ashamed.

Anthony and Honey burst out laughing.

"Relax, man," said Anthony. "We ain't gonna fuck this up. This is just as important for us, maybe more so."

Honey shot Anthony a silencing look.

The two of them got back to work, loading the car, but in a more subdued mood. At eleven-thirty, all three got in the Plymouth and Anthony drove

100

them to the spot they had picked out. It was a short run from the exchange to the car.

They got out and checked their gear. Anthony carried a forty-four, Sean carried two nine millimeter pistols and the smoke grenade and Honey had a three fifty-seven revolver strapped to her waist. She never shot it before and hoped she never would. Sean gave them each a gas mask.

They walked to the other side of the road from the back entrance to the diamond exchange. There, they put on their masks and gloves in the alley.

"We'll go in when I give the signal," said Sean.

Right at midnight, the armored van drove up. A guard came out of a door in the back of the exchange. He went to the driver and they chatted as the guard checked all the paperwork. The guard went over to a service door and rang the bell. The door lifted from the inside and two other guards stood with several black leather bags on the ground between them. The first guard gave the thumbs up to the driver who backed the van up to the service door. The driver and his guard got out and went to the back.

Sean gave the signal. The three of them darted across the street. Honey and Anthony ran up the right side of the van, while Sean ran up the left. He poked his head in the opening of the service door, pulled the pin on the grenade and threw it right into the middle of the five men.

Things blurred after that. The five men scattered as the grenade went off, filling the room with smoke. Honey and Anthony ran in and knocked out the two guards closest to them. Sean took out two more with equal precision. They grabbed the bags and ran back out of the service room.

They ran no more than twenty feet when the last guard came crashing out of the service bay. He yelled for them to stop. Sean whirled around unloading both guns on the guard. The guard took a bullet to the head and his brains splattered the wall and sidewalk like a Jackson Pollack painting.

"What the fuck?" shouted Anthony.

A maniacal grin split Sean's face and lunacy shined in his eyes. "No choice," he said, then turned and ran.

Sean dropped both his guns down a sewer grate as they jumped into the car. Anthony turned the key. The engine sputtered, then gunned to life. They were out so quickly that no one had time to alert the police.

Anthony drove straight back to the warehouse in silence. He eased into the warehouse where they unloaded the gear, leaving the bags of diamonds in the car for Honey to get to the bank. Once everything was accounted for, Anthony walked up to Sean and punched him dead in the mouth.

"Fuck, man," yelled Sean. "What the fuck was that for?"

Anthony went after him again. Honey stepped in between. Anthony backed down. Hone turned on Sean.

"Why did you shoot him?" she yelled, as Sean stood clutching his bloodied mouth. "We had a plan and you went renegade."

"We couldn't take the chance," said Sean slowly. "He had to be taken out."

"You killed him," said Honey, with hate in her eyes. "Cold-blooded murder."

"Look, he knew what could happen in his line of work." Sean smiled, cruel and hard. "Serves him right for not just staying inside. Besides, we got the diamonds. We're home free unless you two open your mouths 'cause sure as shit, I won't be saying anything."

"What makes you think we'd say something?" asked Anthony, barely holding his anger in check.

"Because you have something to lose," said Sean, looking Honey in the eyes and then dropping his gaze to leer at her stomach.

Shaking with rage and humiliation, Honey slapped Sean full on the face. He fell back against the table. In a rage, he grabbed a gun off the table and aimed it at Honey.

"You stupid bitch," he growled.

Anthony sprinted across the floor. Before Sean could make a move, Anthony speared him. They both tumbled to the ground, knocking the gun out of Sean's hands.

They wrestled, neither gaining advantage over the other until Sean threw an elbow into Anthony's eye. Anthony roared in pain, grabbed his eye and let Sean go. Sean scrabbled for the gun. Honey was quicker and kicked him in the jaw, flipping him back into Anthony.

Anthony threw a quick punch into Sean's throat then stood up. Sean recovered quickly, spun around and swept Anthony's feet from under him. Sean scuttled on hands and knees back to the gun. Honey again tried to intercept, but Sean was ready this time. He grabbed her leg in mid-air, throwing her off-balance. He scooped the gun off the floor, but Honey's distraction had cost him too much time. Anthony barreled down on him again.

They threw punches left and right as they tried to gain control of the gun. Anthony yelled for Honey to get help. She just opened the car door when a loud report echoed throughout the warehouse.

Anthony staggered back, holding his stomach. Sean had the gun in his hand. A small curl of smoke rose from the barrel. Anthony turned towards Honey. She screamed when she saw his blood-soaked hands.

"Run," he said through clenched teeth and fell to the floor.

Honey jumped in and gunned the engine. Sean fired twice, shattering the back window as Honey rammed the car through the garage door.

Sean looked down at Anthony, who writhed in agony on the floor.

"I'm going to get your bitch and my diamonds," said Sean, his face a rictus of rage. "The pain you're in now will be nothing compared to what I'm going to do to her."

"Go to hell," said Anthony, breathing heavily.

"You first," said Sean and he pulled the trigger.

***

Anthony sat bolt upright in the driver's seat. His eyes snapped open as he felt the cold bullet pierce his skull. The image of Honey screaming seared into his brain. He knew she had to be found fast. Sean would stop at nothing to make good on his promise to hurt her.

Almost all of Anthony's memories were back. A few missing pieces, but he had enough to find her. He conjured in his mind all of his memories of her. In a flash, it came to him. He knew where she was.

Shortly after they moved in together, but before meeting Sean, they went hiking a lot. On one of their hikes, they found an abandoned cabin. It was in bad shape when they had found it, but they fixed it up. They went there from time to time when they needed to reconnect and just get away from the city. They also buried a lot of their cash there for emergencies. Anthony was sure that is where she would be.

He wound his way through the city, finally hitting the freeway and headed out into the country. It took about a half an hour until he pulled down a one lane dirt road, if it could even be called a road. He and Honey used to pretend it was the driveway to their cabin. Anthony eased the car over the rough road into a small clearing. He saw the Plymouth covered in some brush, its back window shattered.

He parked his car and got out. There was a path about a half mile long that he would need to trek to get to the cabin. He walked the path, noticing that it was eerily quiet. No birds chirped, no wind bent the trees. He remembered a similar calm when he resurrected in the warehouse.

At the end of the path a clearing surrounded the cabin. The log cabin pre-dated running water and electricity. Two rocking chairs sat on the small front porch with a stack of firewood behind them. The chimney poked out of the north side of the roof. Smoke rose lazily out of the chimney now. Another path led to a small lake around the south side of the cabin. Anthony remembered them picnicking down by the water. They always talked about going fishing, but neither of them knew how.

Anthony stopped about ten feet from the porch as a shot rang out and kicked up dirt at his feet. He yelped and jumped back in surprise. Honey stood in the door with a rifle braced against her shoulder.

"Don't come any closer," she said, aiming the muzzle of the rifle at his chest.

Anthony put his hands up, a small smile tugging at his lips. She moved with poise and grace and Anthony couldn't help himself, even facing down the barrel of the gun.

"Hi, Honey," he said, standing very still.

She inched out onto the porch until she stood at the top of the stairs.

"It can't be," she said, her voice shaking. "You're dead. I saw you die."

"I know," he reassured her. "I'm back."

Honey dropped the rifle, ran down the steps and sprinted into his arms. She grasped him so tight he heard his ribs pop, but that didn't stop him from gripping her back just as tight. She tilted her head up and he kissed her, passionately as if the fate of the entire world was at stake.

"How is this possible?" she asked when their lips finally parted.

"Not Heaven or Hell could keep me from you," he said, holding her close. "Did you get the diamonds?"

"I did," replied Honey. "They're inside. What are we going to do with them? Sean had the fence."

"We'll find someone. For now, we have plenty of money stashed."

They turned and went up the porch steps. Anthony held the door open for Honey. Without warning, there was a crack and the wood near his head erupted into splinters. Honey jumped inside while Anthony dropped to the ground.

Sean emerged from the woods into the clearing. He strode quickly toward the cabin holding a pistol in each hand. He stopped abruptly when he recognized Anthony.

"How the hell..." said Sean in a disbelieving voice. "You're a dead man."

"So I've heard," said Anthony.

He quickly picked up the rifle and fired at Sean. Sean dove to the ground crawling to a fallen tree using it for cover. He took a few blind shots back.

Anthony calmly walked down the stairs and took aim at where Sean lay behind the log. Sean heard him coming, quickly sat up and fired again, hitting Anthony in the chest. Sean whooped victoriously and took two more shots, both hitting Anthony. Anthony dropped to the ground, prone.

Grinning from ear to ear, Sean strutted up to the still form of Anthony.

"I got you this time, you son of a bitch," he said with contempt in his voice.

Anthony's eyes flicked open. He raised the rifle and shot Sean in the shoulder. The bullet knocked Sean sideways then down on all fours. Anthony took his time getting up.

"You can't kill me," said Anthony. "I'm already dead."

He took aim at Sean's head. "This is payback, motherfucker."

Before he could pull the trigger, Anthony stumbled as agonizing pain shot through his ankle. He looked down as several worms bore into his leg. He used the butt of the rifle to try to dislodge them, but the pain intensified and he fell to the ground, howling.

Sean saw his chance and fired another round at Anthony, hitting him in the side of the neck. Anthony continued rolling around, trying to pull out the worms. Sean fired again and again, emptying his clips into Anthony's contorting body.

Defying the pain, Anthony allowed the worms to burrow into his body. He grabbed Sean by the pant leg and dragged him to the ground. Anthony rolled on top of him. He opened his mouth wide and heaved, vomiting the worms directly onto Sean's face.

The worms latched onto Sean digging their way into his flesh. Blood sprayed from the gashes. His eyes popped like grapes as worms drilled through them. Anthony slid off as Sean squealed like an animal caught in a trap. He slapped at the worms as they entered his body through one hole and emerged from a new one.

Anthony knew this agony well and took pity on Sean. He took the rifle off the ground, raised it and placed a bullet straight into Sean's heart, sparing him the pain that he had caused Anthony and Honey.

Sean stopped moving as the worms continued their feast. Anthony watched in revulsion. He again saw the ring that seemed familiar to him before. He quickly snatched it from the pile before it disappeared.

He turned from the awful sight and made his way back to Honey. She watched, horrified, from the porch. She buried her head into his shoulder. He stroked her back. After her terror subsided, she looked again at the mangled mess, now more worms than flesh.

"Just what he deserved," she said in a hollow voice.

"I don't think anyone deserves that," said Anthony, shuddering.

He looked down at the ring in his hand. Honey let out a shriek of delight and took it from him.

"What… what is it?" asked Anthony.

"You don't remember?" Honey gave him a hurt look.

"I've got most of my memories, but not all of them," he said trying to explain away the guilt he felt. "They come and go in spurts."

"You do remember I'm pregnant, right?"

Anthony laughed.

"How could I possibly forget that?" he smiled and pulled the pregnancy test from his pocket.

Honey smiled.

"Well," she started, "let me try to remind you then."

She gently took Anthony's left hand and placed the ring on his third finger. Images burst into his mind of a wedding--their wedding.

"We got married?" he asked.

"You insisted," said Honey. "You said this baby had to have a fighting chance in this world and the only way to do that was for us to be married."

Anthony grinned taking Honey's hands in his. Behind him, he heard a rustling noise. They both turned toward the noise, alarmed. The worms finished their meal. Nothing was left of Sean save his clothes and the jewelry he had been wearing. The worms entwined themselves back and forth, picking up the pieces and making it a part of their bulk. When they finished, the horde stopped, as if waiting. A hissing sound emanated from their collective.

Anthony tilted his head, listening. He started visibly shaking and his face clouded.

"No," he said to the mass. "I'm not ready."

The worms whispered back. Anthony shook his head and took a step back. The worms inched forward. Anthony quickly shouldered the rifle and shot twice into the pile. The bullets disappeared for a moment, and then re-emerged as a part of the collective, swirling around with the other items. The worms buzzing got louder, like a mother scolding her misbehaving child.

Anthony's shoulders drooped. He turned to Honey and squeezed her hands.

"I have to go," he said, his voice tired and defeated.

"What? No!" shouted Honey, clutching him tighter. "I need you. Your baby needs you!"

"I know," said Anthony, gripping her, "but I'm dead. What kind of father would that be for our child?"

"A damn good father," she replied, crying.

He laughed. "Damned is right."

He held her for a long time, letting her weep into his shoulder. He kissed her face and head. When her sobbing dwindled, he took her face in his hands.

"I will always love you," he said, his voice choking, "and our child, but I can't stay. If I do, the worms will always find me.

"You're a strong woman and I know that you'll raise our child with everything we never had. You'll love this child like we love each other and you will teach this child to enjoy life. And I know that you will not let this child follow the path that we chose. We both have to pay for that."

Anthony closed his eyes and placed his forehead against Honey's. He kissed her and wiped the tears from her eyes. He pulled himself from her embrace, turned and walked to the worms.

"We have to pay for our mistakes in blood."

He addressed the pile. "Thank you for giving me the chance to see my Honey one last time."

The worms writhed and the hissing became a humming, like a sad lament sung at a funeral.

Anthony blew a kiss to Honey, who grabbed it and placed it on her chest. Anthony lay down on the floor of the forest.

"Ashes to ashes, dust to dust," said Anthony and he closed his eyes.

The worms wriggled over him, covering his entire body. He felt no pain as they began their work. Instead, he went inside his mind and replayed the newfound memory of his wedding.

When the worms were done, they became silent and slowly descended into the earth. Honey walked over to where Anthony's burial had finally taken place and dropped to her knees. The sun broke through the trees and a single ray of light glinted off something on the ground in front of her. With a small smile, she picked up Anthony's wedding ring. She rubbed it between her fingers and placed it in her pocket. She brushed off her hands, stood up and went to the cabin to begin her new life as a mother.

Scree

Sandra Stephens

When Artie called to ask if she'd seen Meggie, his little long-eared dachshund, the feeling that had been bugging Mir stopped tapping on the door of her anxiety, opened it and walked on through. Something was wrong, had been since Norm died. Since before he died.

It started back in April, when Bandelero disappeared. It was Artie's opinion the coyotes got him, but he hadn't seen the remains like Mir had. All that was left of the cat was a few pieces of orange marmalade fur, a bone that might have been a rib and his collar with the blue heart shaped tag. Something had caught him unawares - not an easy thing to do with an old campaigner like Bandy.

Even when Kippy disappeared three months later she still hadn't really cottoned to it. Kippy had come to them a feral stray, but seemed happy enough to join Bandy on the deck during the day and sleep in a cat bed at night. Then. one night, no Kippy; a night stretched into a week, then a month, then a season. She knew if it had been either of their Australian shepherds, Clarita or Mitsy, that went missing Norm would have searched the chaparral and nearby highway day and night until he found them, or whatever remained of them. But Mir couldn't bring herself to look - not after Bandy. And if she had, she'd be dead instead of in Mexico, in a place where she could listen to the sound of the ocean through her open window without fear…for how long, though, was anyone's guess.

***

Artie was Artie Blodgett, Norm's friend and her nearest neighbor, though with Norm gone she guessed Artie was her friend now. Artie lived two miles west from Mir's place as the crow flies, a forty minute hike on a trail that switched back on itself half a dozen times and crossing one creek or a fifteen minute drive on steep winding roads.

Everyone called Artie Blodge, but Mir called him Artie, as she had since third grade. Artie still called her Mira, from their high school days, not remembering (or not caring to remember) how some of the jocks had tormented her with it. "Mira Mira won't come near ya", a dual reference to her virginity and her vague dykeyness, a thing Mir could help no more than she could change her height, or her eye color.

"Go easy on poor Blodge," Norm advised. "That was all a long time ago."

"For your information I *do* go easy on him. I've never said one word about him being literally the only person on earth still calling me *Mira*. He comes over practically every other Sunday. I cook and I do the dishes while he gets loaded and tells war stories."

"Your mom still calls you Mira," Norm had said and ducked away as Mir pretended to slap him.

"You know Artie loves you like a sister. He's just not good at expressing himself."

"Unless he's talking about alien invasions," Mir said. "Then he'll talk your ear off."

"That's when you focus on the love part," Norm said. "And you have to admit some of his theories are ...strangely interesting."

"The only thing strange is how Artie can find the time to research UFOs but not find the time to fix his place up," Mir grumbled.

But when Mir went to the Saturday farmer's market and saw the sign for Meggie, her heart sank. Lost Dog, it read, with a low resolution photo of the miniature dachshund looking absurdly beautiful. REWARD. There were little tear-off strips with Artie's number, none of them torn off yet.

It had been a week since Meggie had disappeared from Artie's back yard, wandering or carried off into the impenetrable deer browse that carpeted Mount Tam. Some dogs might survive out there in the thirsty brush among the bobcats and coyotes, but she feared Meggie would not be one of them. She hoped like hell the dog had found its way down to the valley, maybe wandered into someone's yard. Artie loved that dog like no other.

Artie was gruff about taking the groceries she brought him, but Mir just put the blueberries and romaine in his fridge, giving him no chance to refuse them. She didn't ask if there was news of Meggie, seeing the answer in his slumped shoulders.

"I'll put up a notice on Facebook for her," she told Artie. "Maybe someone has seen something."

She went out to his deck - a project he and Norm had worked on for an entire summer - and opened her laptop.

"Where are m' manners?" asked Artie gruffly. "Coffee? Tea? Beer?"

"Tea," said Mir, without looking up. Artie paused with the screen door opened.

"It's real good to see you, Mira," he said. "I don't get many visitors 'cept someone from PG&E now and then."

She smiled and gave a little "aw go on with you" wave of her hand.

"No, I mean it. You and Norm have been good friends. I woulda lit out for Mexico a long time ago but for you two."

It was quiet on the deck, the sound of the wind small and constant, like a whisper. Clarita found a warm sunny spot and lay down, panting. A squirrel chattered from high up a tree. A single Anna's hummingbird suspended at Artie's feeders, its pink head gleaming in the late afternoon sunlight.

"Where are all your friends?" Mir asked it. The feeders usually buzzed with hummingbird society, it was one of the chief attractions of Artie's place.

A delicious smell gradually filled the air, like cookies baking.

"Artie *baking*? Mir thought, disbelieving. She could even make out individual ingredients - brown sugar, vanilla, cinnamon.

Snickerdoodles! she thought. *That was what they were called - the ones Mom made at Christmas.*

But when Artie came back it was with a longneck for himself and a mug of Lipton tea for her - no cookies, no snickerdoodles, no baked goods of any kind. Before she could question him about the source of the delicious smell he was deep into the latest entry in his logbook. Artie tracked something he called *disturbances*, recording UFOs and Bigfoot sightings - among other things - cross-checking them against news reports of power outages, abductions and missing persons reports, mass killings of fish, missing livestock. Once Mir had asked him what criteria he used to decide if an event was a disturbance.

"Things that shouldn't *be*, but somehow *are*," was the answer.

Norm always listened to Artie's debriefings with respect. "Just because he's a little crazy doesn't mean he isn't a smart guy," he said. Mir remembered the last briefing when Norm was still well - he had sat right here on the deck next to Mir. Artie had opened his journal to the last three pages where his observations were written in a tight, looping script that was surprisingly neat. Copperplate, her mother had called it. Mir thought it was just like Artie to have mastered a lost art like cursive, but not fix the broken window in his laundry room.

"Davey Flaherty said he saw a deer get caught in the sludge over by the water treatment plant." Artie's updates always cited at least one witness, something he was very strict about.

Mir knew one of the idyllic townships right on the peninsula had dumped millions of gallons of

117

sewage into the Bay three years ago and was fined, only to spew twice as many million gallons the next year.

"Did it drown? asked Mir.

"Davey says whatever had the deer took its head clean off and drug it away."

"What?" Mir cried.

"I've read about farm workers overcome by methane, falling into pig manure pits and dying - maybe that's what happened to the deer," Norm speculated, later at home.

"Artie said something dragged the head away." Mir shuddered at the mental picture.

"Well, Martini Dave isn't what you'd call the most reliable witness," was all Norm said and they both laughed, guiltily - Dave wasn't exactly a friend but they'd known him forever. Age made you comrades in arms somehow, Mir thought.

"It does get you thinking sometimes, though," she mused.

"About what?"

"Where it all goes - the stuff from all those oil spills and sewage leaks. It doesn't just disappear."

"Maybe it lies in wait for the unsuspecting," Norm had growled, grabbing at Mir who ran from the kitchen back to the bedroom, mock-screaming and laughing and forgetting all about Artie's logbook.

As Artie talked and Mir remembered, Clarita snoozed on the deck. A breeze blew from the west and scrubbed the smell away and Mir forgot all about it until she was more than halfway home.

At twenty minutes into the hike home, the trail narrowed to a single track. Clarita trotted ahead, occasionally doubling back to check in then racing ahead again. There was a brief burst of music from a car driving the winding Highway 1 below them. Above them the silent crucifix shape of a Cooper's hawk circled like an omen.

Mir marched along, planting her trekking poles and stepping in a rhythm that kept her heart rate high enough to breathe harder without gasping or breaking into an uncomfortable, chilling sweat. She would follow this trail to where it hooked up with an even narrower path known mostly to mountain bikers that would take them up and over the ridgeline. If she kept her pace they'd be home by dark, though she wasn't worried - she had her headlamp, Clarita had her collar light and the way would be easy footing by then.

She knew the trail like the back of her hand; it was a hike she'd made at least once a month for more than a decade. Like herself, the trail was pretty much unchanged in all that time, with the exception that everything was noticeably drier. She was a sturdy looking woman who had been a sturdy looking girl and if she'd lost the smoothness of that girl she could still run like one, maybe slower but by God still running.

The low sage rattled. A fawn scrambled onto the trail, all skinny legs and bulging eyes. It spared them not a glance, not even when Clarita barked with her ears laid back. The fawn headed upslope

119

with a wobbly leap. Clarita sent it on its way with a final bark and disappeared around the next bend of the trail, tail high with the satisfaction of a job well done. Mir smiled. She thought Clarita was not unlike herself, high strung but reliable and fast when she really needed to be.

There was the unmistakable smell of cinnamon. She paused, looking around. It wasn't impossible a cinnamon bush had found its way into the browse, but nowhere did she see the telltale tiny purple and white clusters of flowers.

Downslope in the deer's wake, the low brushy sage shook. A puff of dust rose. As Mir watched, the shaking moved closer, another puff of dust rising. The third puff rising snapped her out of her passivity. Whatever was chasing the fawn had changed its vector and was now heading straight for Clarita.

Mountain lion! she thought and broke into a run. She would feel it in her thighs tomorrow, but for now she felt the effortless fleetness that a pure adrenaline dump brings.

"Clarita!" she shouted as she ran. The path bent left then right, the embankment rising on one side, falling away on the other. She thought Clarita must be near the mountain bike path turnoff.

"Clarita, NOW!" She was screaming, something Norm never did. Of course with Norm the dogs were respectful and prompt. When it came to Mir they cheerfully obeyed her when it suited them.

120

"Be patient, trust their judgment," Norm had tried to tell her. "If you really need them, you won't have to call them twice."

As if in proof, Clarita's narrow, intelligent black and white face hove into view, on the run. Adrenaline and pride burst through Mir.

She flung one of her trekking poles, javelin-like. It flew at an angle downhill. The next puff of dust and rattle of sage followed it.

"Go, go, go!" she told Clarita, pitching her voice low. Clarita bounded away.

Mir whipped the second trekking pole around her head by the handle strap until the air hummed. It flew a good hundred yards downslope from the first pole. Immediately the sage rattled and rolled after it.

Mir kept her eyes glued to the ground just in front of her foot plants as she ran, serpentining back and forth across the path as it steepened. Running downhill fast without killing herself was a skill she had picked up in high school cross country, racing on these very trails. This one would dump them into a small dirt parking lot at the side of the highway.

The lot usually contained one or two cars, or bikers or runners enjoying the shade, but today it was empty when Clarita shot like a black and white arrow into its center, barking. Mir was fifteen yards away, still careful with her footing as the slope flattened and became slippy with leaves and pebbles when she heard the underbrush shifting and shaking directly behind her.

She ran into the empty dirt arena where Clarita stood barking but nothing burst from the bushes - no bobcat, no mountain lion, no coyotes. The shaking came right up to the edge of the woods and stopped, a dozen yards from where Mir and Clarita stood panting. Mir couldn't see whatever it was but felt reassured - there wasn't enough cover for a mountain lion or a big cat.

The warm smell of baking cookies filled the clearing.

She heard a whimper, barely glimpsing the rounded top of a little forehead with silky brown ears before it backed into the brush again.

"Meggie!" Mir cried and started forward. At the last second she saw what was really in the brush and skidded to a halt.

The ground rose up, robed in scree and scrub and crowned with the top half of poor Meggie's head, all that was left of the friendly little brown dachshund.

Mir stumbled backward, falling. Her palms hit the ground hard and she crabbed backward frantically, the gravel cutting her hands. Clarita darted in front of her, barking crazily.

"Clarita no! Get back!" Mir screamed.

The goo surged and rolled forward, a wave of liquefied earth stippled with brush and gravel, bits of broken glass and animal bones. Mir saw the bedraggled tail of a squirrel, the carcasses of birds, individual wings and feet and beaks all stuck in a dust-coated goo.

It reached forward in long fat fingers like the surf on the sand at Rodeo Beach, wearing rings of sticks and stones instead of foam.

Clarita barked and barked.

"Clarita, COME," Mir shouted. In slow motion, Mir watched as the thing sent a scree-covered pseudopod to strike Clarita squarely on her furry white chest.

"NO!" she screamed, but it was already too late. The pseudopod bisected itself to collar the little shepherd's neck. Clarita's bark was a single, startled pained yelp.

Mir turned her head aside with a cry but not before she saw blood pour in a freshet down Clarita's crisp white bib. It dripped onto the surface of the goo where it danced like oil on a skillet before simply sinking into the thing, absorbed with a kind of slurping sound.

There was the sound of gravel stones clicking together as it sent fingers creeping forward again, toward the sound of Mir's cry.

She gained her feet and backed up slowly, keeping her eyes on the advancing rim of the scrub. The odor of vanilla was powerful now, bringing confused thoughts of Sperry's Bakery she'd visited with her dad on Sundays when she was a kid; the sweet smell of the donuts so thick in the air you could almost taste it. A smell that made her want to stand still, sampling it from the air, remembering things like the way her dad always got one glazed twist donut and one old-fashioned and got Mir two blueberry cake donuts and a bear claw for her mother who would eat only half and frown at Mir when she ate the other half.

While she stood there lost in memory the finger thinned, spreading itself flat on the ground. Reaching.

123

Another wave of that delicious vanilla scent. *Mir, take those cookies out, will you.*

She took a step forward, then another. *Mama would be mad if the cookies burned,* she thought.

A sudden blast of Bon Jovi hit her as a car wound its way past on Highway 1.

Mir took a deep breath and held it, breaking the spell of smell. She walked backwards in quick, quiet steps until she felt the heel of her hiking boot hit the smooth composition surface of Highway One.

The thing didn't move. Now it looked like any other small patch of scree, something any hiker would unthinkingly scuff though.

Mir ran, snapping glances over her shoulder, but the road behind her remained empty. She didn't breathe until she was fifty yards down the hill. Her legs shook as reaction set in and she forced herself to slow to a fast walk. *No sense getting away from that thing and then having a stroke*, she thought.

That brought her to a full stop.

She had thought Norm's bulging- eyed post-stroke stare was a result of his brain injury. When he'd first stumbled into the yard, his left arm already a stiffening block of useless wood, his expression had looked urgent. His mouth had worked, but only garbled syllables came out. The pupil of his left eye had grown large and fixed, like a round oil spill in a lake of glacial blue.

She had assumed he was trying to tell her about his stroke, which had paralyzed his smart hand and leg - his whole left side really, plus his mouth and vocal cords. But maybe he'd been trying to tell her something he'd seen out there.

The lights of the Chevron gas station market at the foot of the hill looked both festive and surreal in the fast-falling twilight, the shoppers calmly paying for their Cheetos and gas like actors, not even looking up as the bell above the door tinkled when Mir entered with her wide, shocked eyes, like Jimmy Stewart in it's a Wonderful Life.

She felt strongly that she should stay something, but what? *The ground rose up and ate my dog* wasn't the kind of thing you could just announce. Everyone would just stare at her, maybe give embarrassed smiles instead of racing home to pack and leave, go far away from a thing that could do such a thing, the only rational reaction.

Mir held it together long enough to call a cab. She didn't start sobbing until the cab passed the parking lot, still empty, still strewn with fingers of scree and no Clarita in sight, the cab driver eyeing her with a combination of discomfort and curiosity in his rearview mirror.

***

At home she put food down for Mitsy, but Mitsy wouldn't eat. She looked around for Clarita, staring at Mir and whimpering.

When she couldn't put it off any longer, Mir called Artie. As usual he let the answering machine screen the call.

"Artie, it's Miranda," she said after the beep. "I… I know what happened to Meggie." She thought of poor Meggie's mutilated head, Clarita's final yelp. Her throat closed with tears. She paused, trying to steady herself.

"It got Clarita, too."

Artie picked up. "Mountain lion?" His voice slurred a little, she thought.

"It happened at the trailhead. I think it's better if I tell you in person," she said. "I'll come over tomorrow."

She sat unseeing in front of the television, the sound on mute, a habit she'd picked up after Norm died. She couldn't sleep, even if she hadn't been drinking coffee sitting on the couch watching the moon cross the sky. There was Mitsy to reassure for one thing. She lay with her head in Mir's lap; at every movement Mir made, the dog raised her head, her gaze going from Mir's face to the sliding glass doors and back again, her question "Where's Clarita?" plain as day.

"I'm sorry, girl," Mir told her, scratching behind her ears. It didn't comfort either of them.

She couldn't shake the thought that maybe Norm had seen the thing, tried to tell her - and not just the day of the stroke. She remembered a day she'd held the binoculars up to zoom in on an elk standing in the middle of the door yard, calmly chewing. It was the kind of thing she did on the regular, bringing Norm's chair to the window and putting the binoculars to his eyes, pressing her cheek to his so she could adjust them properly so he could see: the hummingbirds at the feeders, a coyote - a big handsome brute of a fellow - sitting at the edge of the woods watching Clarita and Mitsy watching him from behind the sliding glass doors. A butterfly migration passing through, turning the air to confetti.

The day of the elk Norm had tilted his head back, knocking the binoculars with his chin so that the glasses were pointed at the hills above the elk. She started to readjust and he knocked the glasses with his chin again, staring hard at her. Mir put her eye to the glasses, where they pointed to the mountain beyond the elk, a slope called Christmas Tree Hill.

It was so big she had almost missed it, even though she was looking right at it.

A section of the northwestern slope of the hill was moving in a slow-motion landslide. It was as if everything - bushes, rocks, trees and the ground itself - rode on a surfboard riding a gently undulating wave that continued even after the slope leveled off.

"Whoa, earthquake!" Mir said. But there was no telltale rumbling beneath their feet. She looked over the top of the glasses, trying to see it with her own eyes... but by then the ground out there was still.

Norm had made one of the few sounds he was able to make, at great effort, holding her eyes insistently with his good one. Had he been trying to show her that thing, tell her he'd seen it before?

She readied herself for bed as usual, the feeling of surreality recurring. Was she really going to just brush her teeth while the thing that took Clarita was out there?

She was.

She flossed and swished a swish of mouthwash for thirty seconds, turning the inside of her mouth into an empty cave of burning mint. The thought she'd been pushing down all evening broke free, drifting to the front of her consciousness.

"You're going to have to report it," she told her reflection. Behind her, Mitsy lifted her head in hope - *are we going to get Clarita now?* - then lay back down with a sigh.

"It could get a person, maybe." But she wasn't sure she believed that.

She climbed into bed, her hips aching a little from the sprinting. Tomorrow that ache would be more pronounced, she knew.

If she tried to tell anyone, they would treat her like a crazy old lady who lived alone, slowly going off her rocker. They'd call her a Karen.

She turned on her side to face the double glass doors which opened onto the deck with its view of the sunrise. Tonight the moon rode like an indifferent white eye high in a sky thick with stars.

She heard the jingle of Mitsy's collar as she curled up on the living room couch where she was keeping watch for Clarita, giving the occasional whimper in her sleep.

Mir felt like she'd never sleep again. This was different from the grief that stole her sleep for months after Norm died. This was a wide-awake nerviness, her body still retaining the memory of the adrenaline that had slammed through her and sent her flying down the mountain. The shock when it took Clarita.

She didn't doubt for a second what she'd seen, or question her sanity. She knew what she saw, no matter how impossible it seemed.

"But what the fuck WAS it?" she muttered aloud. She was not surprised when Norm's voice came out of the dark in response. She'd been imagining his voice in her head since he died - since the stroke, really. It helped her think through things.

"Well, what did it look like?" Questioning *her*, as in *tell me what you saw* and not *questioning* her, as in are *you sure you saw that or maybe you saw something else* like she knew everyone else would, like they'd been doing ever since she passed the Rubicon of sixty-five.

"It looked like *nothing*. It looked like the ground, or something pretending to be the ground. Like the ground itself took her."

"I'm sorry I lost her," she choked. The silence behind her was just as it would have been in Norm's life - he was quiet when his mom died and his sister. This made her cry harder, not for Clarita but for herself. Norm really was gone, she knew. No matter how many tricks she played with his voice in her head, it was just the melatonin kicking in, not Norm.

Just as she dropped off, she felt Mitsy leap onto the bed and assume her normal spot at the foot of Norm's side.

Good girl.

She was almost asleep when his voice came out of the dark.

Maybe that's what got all the birds.

***

In the morning Mir sat with Mitsy on the deck, having her coffee and steeling herself to go to Artie's and tell him - what, exactly? *The ground killed Meggie?*

She saw Norm's field glasses (what he'd always called his birdnoculars) in their usual spot, hanging on the peg beneath the rail. She put them to her eyes and adjusted them with a little pang - no matter what happened, they'd never be adjusted to Norm's vision ever again.

The feeders they'd installed throughout the property - usually a haven for bushtits and scrub jays and the occasional pileated woodpecker - stood quiet. She couldn't remember the last time she saw a family of little crowned quail scurrying at the scrubby edges of the trail.

Against her will Mir remembered the way the goo had elongated, leaping through the air to lasso Clarita. It was easy enough to picture it snagging a bird unawares… at least until the birds became aware enough to leave.

She'd thought turkey vultures had gotten to Bandy but when was the last time she had seen a turkey vulture, or wild turkeys, for that matter?

She scanned the line of the woods where it marched up to the edge of their property line on the west edge. Big bumble bees hovered over the white death lilies and star tulips and orange bush poppies. Nothing swayed the cypress; the lupine lay undisturbed. The manzanita moved not at all.

Then, in the magnified gaze of the binoculars, there was a commotion in the chaparral oak. Mir's heart jumped, then settled as a black tailed doe stepped into the yard, looked around and lowered her head to nibble at some acorns.

Mitsy watched the deer but with no great enthusiasm - not without Clarita. There were almost always crows in the trees at the edge of the property, loud and sassy. A mockingbird had mimicked the sound of the wooden screen door slamming all summer - she hadn't heard it in weeks.

The high nerviness was still singing in her veins. It was time to go to Artie's, tell him Meggie was indubitably gone.

Normally she left the sliding glass doors between the living room and the deck open, so the dogs could go in and out at will. Today she shut them firmly. Mitsy whined.

"You're going to stay safe right here," she whispered to Mitsy's bright little eyes looking back at her. She smoothed her furry ears. "I'll be back soon."

She looked back from the door between the kitchen and the garage. The sliding glass doors diffused the sunlight that fell on the couch, the coffee table, the lamp and the bookshelves. In the elegiac light they looked like relics.

The thought rose like a balloon, unbidden. *When you're gone it will look just like this. Like you and Norm were never here.*

She slammed the door, breaking the quiet.

131

***

When she pulled into his driveway Artie knew right away something was up. Mir was a spry woman and walked or rode a bike instead of driving to Artie's as a point of pride and never went anywhere without her dogs if it could be helped. Now here she was, poochless and driving the old 4Runner.

"Knee acting up?" he asked as Mir winced her way up the steps to the back deck. She nodded.

"I went on an unexpected run yesterday," she said, easing herself into one of Artie's rickety Adirondacks. "From whatever took Meggie… and Clarita."

"Damn," Artie said. "Jesus, I'm sorry, Mira. Was it coyotes?" He said it the country way, two syllables, like "eye oats" with a k.

Mir shook her head and felt the tears rise.

"I spent most of the night wondering what I was going to tell you, because it sounds so crazy. So I'm just going to tell you. Leave it to you to believe me or not. And if you don't, I won't blame you. I'm not sure I would believe me."

"Well, now you got me interested, anyways," Artie said.

She told him the whole story, starting with the fawn, the throwing of the walking sticks, the way the thing had headed for Clarita. How the ground surged and rolled then rose up. He nodded as she described the elongated fingers becoming a noose for poor Clarita.

132

"It… it took her head right off, Artie," she whispered. "It happened so fast. I couldn't save her."

She took a few deep breaths for what she had to say next, what she knew Artie was waiting for.

"I could see … other things it killed, stuck in it. A squirrel. Some birds. And Meggie… well, what was left of her." She looked at him with huge eyes. "I'm so sorry, Artie."

She hated how old he suddenly looked, how defeated. Though he knew better, she saw he had held out hope he'd get Meggie back.

She excused herself to go to the bathroom, giving him time to pull himself together. She rinsed her face; in the mirror a woman that looked uncomfortably like her mother stared back at Mir. Her mother had called in her condolences over Norm from a cruise ship vacation.

At least he had time and warning enough to get right with God before he went, she told Mir. *I can't remember are you a member of a church out there in California? Church is a great way to meet a nice man. You're not getting any younger, you know.*

As if she needed any reminders that she would probably end up an old woman dying alone, all the proof she had ever been well-loved - by Norm, her cats, Clarita - swallowed by the earth itself

By the time she returned to the deck Artie had blown his nose and wiped his eyes. "You okay, Mira?" he asked gruffly.

"No," she said and uttered a laugh. "But thanks for believing me."

"You may have noticed I ain't so hard to convince as some people," he said. They sat quietly on the deck in their new Meggie-less, Clarita-less world.

"You should get some sleep, Mira," Artie said. "You look tired, if you don't mind me saying so."

She smiled at that. She looked ancient, not unlike Artie himself. *Two old-timers, we are,* she thought. It had happened so much sooner than she thought it would.

"I don't mind what's true. I *am* tired," she agreed, standing to go. "Anything I can bring you from town? Knee replacement, maybe?"

Artie scoffed at her little joke but she knew from the way he used his cane all the time now that his knees were a constant hurt.

"I'm getting around fine and I got enough saved to check into a care home if it comes to that," Artie had told her a while back. "But personally I'm hoping to die in my sleep, no muss, no fuss."

Except for the person who finds you, Mir had thought but didn't say, knowing in all likelihood that person would be her.

"Naw, I'm fine. You take care of yourself now, Mira. And before you bite my head off it ain't me saying it. I'm saying it for Norm. He said if anything ever happened to him, I was to look after you. It's a promise I mean to keep."

Inwardly, Mir rolled her eyes. Artie could barely look after himself but she wasn't going to be the one to point this out to him. The hideous sight of Meggie's excavated head made her feel protective of Artie. She was glad it was something he'd never have to see. Her voice was gentle when she spoke.

"You're not the only one who made Norm a promise. Now substitute some of those beers for water or tomato juice and I'll bring you some tamales from the market next Saturday."

When she backed down the driveway and lifted her hand before pulling into the road he lifted his in return, neither having any clue it was for the last time.

***

Mitsy was pathetically glad to see her, sitting insistently close to Mir while she watched the news and ate a bowl of canned soup heated up in the microwave. The lead story was an Amber Alert for Baby Sherilyn, a six year old who had disappeared from a Scenic Lookout parking lot off Highway One. On the program, drones scoured the rocky cliff side.

Mir had the sliding glass doors open to the mild California breeze with the occasional waft of night jasmine that grew along the deck. Next to her, Mitsy trembled lightly, as if someone had turned up her idle while Mir was at Artie's.

"It's okay, Mits," she told her. "We'll go to the beach tomorrow."

At the word beach Mitsy perked up a little. The trembling became intermittent. When the news ended Mir hit the pause button. It was too early for bed but she went through her ablutions in the bathroom just for the comforting routine of them.

135

Mitsy followed her, watching from the doorway, then went to the bedroom and jumped on the bed, staring at Mir.

"You're not going to make me sleep in here alone are you?" her look seemed to say. Mir lay next to her for a while, until she finally stopped trembling. She felt guilty, knowing Clarita was gone and knowing how, knowing Misty somehow knew but not knowing what to say.

The feeling of high nerviness was there, more insistent than ever. Her blood buzzed like the sound of those drones scouring for Baby Sherilyn.

You have to report it.

No one would believe her.

Doesn't matter. What if that little girl isn't missing at all but stepped on the scree thing, like a mouse in a glue trap? What if the scree thing just rolled her up snug as a bug in a rug?

But that was miles away. Surely the thing couldn't move that fast.

Maybe there isn't just one. Maybe it split itself.

I'll sound crazy.

If not Baby Sherilyn now, then someone else soon. Can you live with that?

Thinking these thoughts, sleep finally overtook her, but there was no peace there either. She dreamt that someone was standing in the dooryard, tossing pebbles so that they hit the bedroom sliding glass doors. *Tick. Tick. Tick.* Her dream self went to the door and saw it was Artie, clad in pajamas and throwing cookies like a diabetic Romeo. Dream Artie shouted, his voice indistinct through the glass. She tried tugging the door open but it wouldn't

136

slide. The cookies kept ticking against the glass and she became annoyed, turning her back to the window. That's when she noticed Mitsy on the bed, haunches raised, teeth bared. She growled and leaped, not at Mir but past her. Mir whirled to see her mother with a plate of snickerdoodles.

You better eat these, her dream mom told her. *You're not getting any younger and you'll need your strength.*

Mir woke curled on her right side, facing the Normless side of the bed and the wall beyond. Mitsy was awake, trembling like a small motor that shook the bed. Moonlight streamed in, casting a crisp shadow of the sliding glass doors onto the wall.

She opened her mouth to reassure Mitsy when her breath caught in her throat: on the shadow wall, something was filling in the moon-limned outline of the patio doors, like dark water filling an aquarium of light. As she watched, long fingers stretched upward, the mass surging behind it, the fingers stretching again.

There was a rattle of pebbles hitting the deck. Mitsy growled. Mir rolled over, the smell of cinnamon strong. For a confused second she wondered if she had already woken up or was still dreaming.

The scree-covered goo from the trailhead was pressed against the window, fully covering the lower third of the expanse of thank God-double-paned glass.

She watched as the goo spread fingers upward and sideways. She heard the slight squeaking sound it made against the window.

It looked bigger than it had at the trailhead. Thicker.

The thought rose before she could stop it. *That's because it ate Clarita.*

By the looks of it, it had eaten a whole platoon of Claritas.

It sent fingers slipping around the door frame, seeking purchase. The door was latched, the piece of wood she kept on the track to foil anyone from opening the door from the outside firmly in place.

The goo extended itself higher. The room darkened as it blotted out more of the bright moonlight. It stretched across the surface of the glass, pulsing and rolling like the surface of a self-contained ocean. Rocks, sticks and bottle caps appeared and disappeared, clicking and scraping against the window. Chunks of fur trailed bloody threads. A kid's sneaker, the kind with the light-up sole. The sole glowed blue with the pressure of the goo filling the inside.

There was a flash of bone in the moonlight, the gleaming white skull and elongated jaw of some small animal pressed up against the window. The moonlight was so bright Mir could clearly see the fissures spread across the surface of the skullcap, first cracking then crumbling into splinters and chunks the size of marbles.

The goo thing was pressing inward, against the glass, hard enough to crush bone. Mir held her breath; would the frame hold?

Beside her, Mitsy growled again, still shaking like a leaf. How long had she been like that while Mir slept? Long enough for the goo to surge through the brush, sending out fingers to pull itself along, crossing the forty yards of their back property, surging up the stairs of the deck and over the railing to plaster itself against the window, looking for a way in.

If the doors had been open, she'd be dead but for Mitsy.

The goo visibly pulsed, the bones pressed up against the window now pulverized into tiny pebbles. She heard the nails on the wood shingles on the house groan and squeal as the thing fanned out, forcing its fingers between them.

A smell of vanilla filled the room.

You left the living room doors open.

The thought was barely formed before she leapt from the bed, bare feet hitting the thick pile of the gabbah they'd brought home from Morocco, then the shock of the cool polished concrete floor of the hallway, then the slick polished walnut of the living room where moonlight flooded through the glass doors. The door to the right was cracked open five inches. The ooze had already sent an investigative tentacle to the leftmost door.

Mir hit the sliding door with the full momentum of her running; for a wonder it didn't stick as usual but slid smoothly on its track, closing with a thump. The snap of the latch and the rattle of the wooden doorstop sounded flimsy, no match for the hundred fingers that shot from the thing, striping the room in moonlight and shadow.

A small rain of pebbles and leaves *and dear God were those teeth?* fell from its surface as it stretched.

The lower fingers merged into a rising tide where drowned and dead things turned. A tangle of rat tails pressed briefly against the glass and was rolled back into the mass with a slurp.

It *was* bigger, she saw. Much, much bigger.

Mir backed slowly away, putting the couch between her and the doors. She moved down the hallway to the bedroom, where the goo was now thinner looking, its upward progress stayed. The glass no longer groaned in its frame under pressure.

But even as she watched, the goo began piling itself back onto the glass. Tiles thunked onto the deck.

Mitsy barked. At the sound, the goo gathered itself into a muscular shape and sucked at the glass like a mouth, at the same level Mitsy stood.

It knows we're in here, she thought. *It hears us, senses us. Something.*

She ran to the kitchen, grabbed a cookie sheet and a metal spoon and banged them together. The goo plastered against the left-handed glass door surged, thickened. From the bedroom Mitsy barked; in response the goo in the living room sent a pseudopod.

Bigger though it was, there wasn't enough of it to mount strong pressure on both doors. If she and Mitsy could stay split up, making noise, the goo would split up, losing strength as it spread itself thin searching for a way in. It wasn't much of a plan but it was better than nothing.

140

She could call the police, of course. And of course they'd come out and of course by then she would either be dead and consumed by the goo, or - and this was much more likely - the goo would be gone and she would be trying to tell them about it. They would be unfailingly polite but she would be able to sense the hilarity already birthed in their bellies, hilarity they'd deliver in the privacy of their squad car.

What do you *think* it was, Mrs. Bailey? they'd ask her in pretend seriousness. They'd ask her if she lived by herself, if she had anyone looking after her.

In the dark of the living room, the answering machine light blinked red. There was only one person who ever called her landline; indeed, she kept it active just for Artie, so he'd have someone to call if he needed help. She'd tried to give him her mobile number a thousand times and he always pretended to take it but she knew he'd never call it.

"Least I know I'm not bothering you when I call the machine," he'd say.

She pressed the button. The sound of breathing filled the room, ragged and gasping.

"It's here, Mira." Artie's voice, hoarse from too much smoking and too many beers. He sounded scared, something she'd never thought possible. But something else in his voice. Was it excitement?

"Came right up between the boards on the deck, covered m' gun and drug it off. I threw my cane like you did your poles. It didn't even hit the ground - it caught it, Mira, right in mid-air. *It just grew an arm and caught it.* I barely made it inside. Been under siege an hour now. If you get this, bring water

- squirt bottles, your CamelBak. Squirt guns, hell, *buckets*. It doesn't like to get wet, Mira."

Artie paused, his breathing still hard. There was a distant sound of breaking glass.

"It's coming in through the laundry; the window in there's been cracked for awhile, dammit. *Dammit.*"

He paused again, trying to catch his breath.

"I'm going to try to trap it in there. If… if you don't get this in time, don't worry, Mira. You been a good neighbor and a better friend."

Another pause, his breathing heavy but even, steeled with a resolve that brought a flood of tears to Mir's eyes.

"I'll see you if I see you. And if I don't, well I'll tell old Norm you said hello." A pause. "I shoulda went to Mexico, dammit."

The receiver clunked on the counter. She found she could track the sounds on the tape easily enough - after all she had been in Artie's house dozens if not hundreds of times.

There was the sound of foot thuds on the broad plank pine floor of his kitchen - she could hear him dragging his bad foot a little, the one with the infection. He yelled, his voice triumphant.

"You'll never take me alive, coppas!"

She knew what he was holding in his hand as he shouted - a Super Soaker, one of those giant squirt guns that looked like a space age long gun . He'd brought two of them over for Norm's sixtieth birthday. Mir had thrown a soiree with party lights strung around the deck, everyone dressed in summer finery. Norm was handsome in a white

142

dinner jacket with an orange poppy as boutonniere. She had floated around in her for-best white silk shawl with a flower in her hair and was feeling almost pretty when Artie had hit her with a blast of water, not just a glancing spray but a full on, up-and-down soaking, laughing hysterically like it was the greatest joke in the world.

"Stop it right now!" she had screamed - really screamed - at Artie. But he was drunk and hilarious, beyond reach.

"You'll never take me alive, coppas!" he had shouted, laughing so hard he fell, hard, on his arm. In the silence after Mir's scream. There was a clean wet snapping sound, Then Artie started to howl, effectively ending the party.

On the tape, a clattering sound after the breaking glass; Artie had dropped the empty? jammed? SuperSoaker as the goo pursued him down the hallway. Artie yelling distantly. A rapid uneven thud-thudding, the shouting growing louder - Artie running back to the kitchen yelling. There was the sound of water running; he must have turned the kitchen tap on.

Get out of here, you fucking moving pile of sewage. Jesus what the fuck... What are you some kind of bp oil spill. Motherfuckers. Ah shit. Ah, God. Je-

His voice cut off with a loud thud, as though he'd fallen. Then the indescribable but unmistakable sounds of the ooze consuming Artie, who returned to consciousness when his ribs collapsed in succession like a xylophone one two three four five six seven eight nine ten eleven twelve. He moaned and then screamed a mercifully brief scream that cut off with a gargling sound.

There was a rapid thud-thud-thud that on second playing Mir knew must be Artie's head bouncing on the uncarpeted wood floor of the hallway he'd only just run down. The thing was retreating - from the water, she guessed - with what was left of Artie in tow.

The head thuds were followed by the metallic hollow bongings of the washer and dryer as it dragged Artie up and over them. A distant sound of splintering wood as his big body was compressed through the tiny window above the washer and dryer. Then nothing but the continuous sound of water overflowing the kitchen sink onto the floor, until the tape cut out.

Now here it was plastered against her sliding glass doors. Seeking a way in.

She filled the watering can, water glasses and serving bowls, lining them up in front of the sliding glass doors and beneath every window. If it did manage to come in, it would have to cross a moat first.

The goo rolled against the window, which creaked in its frame. The naked wishbone of a radius and ulna connected by a metal screw crested to the glass front, skeletal fingers still wrapped around the head of Artie's black cane. *I can go crazy now*, Mir thought. *No one would blame me.*

Norm's voice spoke up in her head, quiet and authoritative.

Fill the tub, it said. Mir groaned aloud at her stupidity. Why create a moat when she could sit in one? She moved quickly, turning on the taps and plugging the sinks in the kitchen and laundry room, pausing to grab Norm's SuperSoaker. In the master bath, she turned both taps to full blast and climbed into the tub with the trembling Mitsy. She dunked the plastic gun, filling the water chamber and pointing it toward the door. She didn't have long to wait.

There was a sound of breaking glass, followed by the ting of a metal bowl flipping over. It was coming in through the kitchen window. It would flow down the sill, encounter the sink full of water, maybe retreat upward to travel around the room via the tops of the kitchen cabinets.

The tub overflowed, water pouring from the curved edge onto the wooden floors she'd once spent an entire weekend stripping and sanding with sheets of 80 grit by hand.

The smell of vanilla filled the room.

Maybe that's how it catches its prey, she had time to think. *Smelling like something you remember. Something nice.*

Mir held her breath. She raised the Soaker, aiming it at the doorway. Still she wasn't ready when the goo surged through the doorway, wasn't ready for it to rise most of the way to the ceiling in a column of scree hideously topped with Clarita's black and white face, wasn't ready for her empty eye sockets to be filled with goo that leaped toward the tub in twinned pseudopods with a blurred speed so fast she barely had time to react. She depressed the trigger of the Soaker using both hands, leaving Mitsy free to leap, snarling at the killer of Clarita.

145

"Mitsy no!" she screamed but Mitsy launched herself without hesitation. Mir felt the strong push of the dog's hind legs as she sailed almost vertically into the air, her muzzle wrinkled back. Mir hit the pseudopods with a fat stream of water and they drooped away from Mitsy's snapping jaw. Elation washed through her, too soon. As Mitsy's leap reached its apex and she began her return trip to the safety of Mir and the water, as Mir dunked the Soaker to refill the chamber a section of the goo bulged forward like a head - Artie's head, in fact, his skull wrapped in goo, a facsimile assembled in scree-covered ooze.

The Artie head's mouth opened and the goo lashed out like some monstrous tongue, spearing Mitsy neatly in midair. Mir screamed, streaming the Soaker at the Artie-thing. Under the fat stream of water it collapsed and thinned and retreated all at once, stretching away from the water and shrinking itself around the inert form of Mitsy even as it pulled itself backward. It retreated out the bathroom door and down the hall, dragging the weight of Mitsy through the dining room and over the kitchen island, over the sink and smashing out what remained of the window in a final hail of broken glass.

For a long time - minutes? hours? - there was no sound but running water. Mir lay in the tub long enough for her fingers to turn pruney and white, for her cheek pressed against the sloped edge of the tub to go numb.

Somewhere on the safe east coast, morning was breaking. But here on the western side of the

146

country the sky was still dark, the last of the night holding hard.

It might come back. It could come down through the ceiling.

She knew nobody would believe her story; everyone who might have believed her was gone, and anyway even she wouldn't believe her story. As soon as they heard about a thing that took a grown man and a toddler, they'd start focusing on the missing grown man, not as the taken but the taker - that's what Mir thought.

The thought got her going. She stood, droplets raining down, feeling naked and exposed without the womb-like protection of the water. She dried herself hurriedly, her thighs still damp as she tugged up her jeans, her sports bra sticking and twisting on her back. Her hands and knees shaking not just from cold and damp but knowing the thing could even now be stuffed inside the chimney, ready to flow out and find her.

She packed quickly, wallet, passport, backpack with an extra pair of jeans and a sweatshirt, hat and windbreaker. After a moment, her red one piece swimsuit with the high cut legs. She did not even glance at the section of her closet that held her dresses and high heels.

No one would raise the alarm about her, or Artie, for a couple of days. There might be an investigation, there might not - water damage was not evidence of foul play, after all. The broken windows might be chalked up to kids, raccoons or bears.

147

Maybe people would talk, say the two of them had run off to Mexico, like Artie was always threatening to do. She found she didn't mind. Artie deserved a better ending than he got.

At the door communicating between the kitchen and the garage she looked back, like she had earlier in the week but now felt like a year ago. Her gaze fell on the kitchen chair where Norm had sat laughing, looking handsome in his white sport coat and the top button of his shirt undone, her with her hair still wet from the soaking Artie had given her.

A piece of glass dropped from the shattered kitchen window into the sink, making her jump. She slammed the door without looking back.

By early evening she had made it to San Diego and checked in at a La Quinta. As she carried her things from the car into her hotel room, she noticed a little boy watching.

"What are you going to shoot with that?" he asked, his longing eyes on the Soaker.

"An oil spill," said Mir.

"Where is it?" asked the boy.

"It could be anywhere," Mir told him. "That's why I have it." She aimed the Soaker at the dense hedge of lantana that grew along the fence around the hotel pool, sending a stream of water along its ten foot length.

"Nope, no oil spill," said Mir.

The boy grinned in delight. "Can I shoot an oil spill?" He pronounced it "thpill".

"Yes," Mir told him. "You can. But you'll need your own weapon. The oil spills are *everywhere*. Can you handle that?"

The boy nodded seriously and put his thumb in his mouth. He was about the age of Baby Sherilyn, Mir guessed.

"But where do I get one?" the boy asked.

"Ask your parents," Mir told him. "Where are they?"

The boy turned to look at one of the motel doors opening onto the same balcony as Mir's. The door was ajar maybe a quarter way.

"Go ahead," she told him. "Go ask, I'm sure they'll say yes."

The boy ran back to his room, bare feet slapping on the concrete. Mir watched, knowing the lantana would not unfurl a tendril, grab him, pull him in and swallow him in a matter of seconds. Still she watched until the door was shut behind him, her heart pounding. The curtain opened briefly; a man looked out, scowling at her.

She found she couldn't sleep until she climbed into the bathtub, the SuperSoaker next to her loaded and ready to go. She pointed it at the doorway, where neither Clarita nor Mitsy sat watch.

"You'll never take me alive, coppas," she whispered in her best sounds-like-Artie voice, then laughed so loud and so long someone from the front desk knocked on her door to tell her there had been a complaint, could she please keep the noise down.

In the morning she went to the hotel's breakfast suite where she picked the shell off a hard-boiled egg and drank black coffee, nearly screaming when the vanilla-heavy smell of freshly made waffles filled the room.

A man with a plate containing only sausages shuffled past, his faded red tank top the same color as his sunburnt slab arms. He gave Mir a double take.

"I'll thank you not to tell my kid what I need to buy him," he snarled. "He won't shut up about that stupid squirt gun."

Mir stared at him, a man about the size of Artie. She remembered the sound Artie's ribs made as they burst apart: crack! crack! crack! crack!

"Just trying to be a good neighbor," she told him.

"Yeah well Christmas ain't for three months, lady. Mind your beeswax."

"I'll do that," Mir told him.

"Fucking loony," he muttered, shuffling away.

She returned to her room and packed her car, the little boy watching her from his window. Mir caught his eye then gave the bushes another good soaking. The boy laughed. Mir gave him a thumbs'-up. The boy stole a glance over his shoulder; a tiny thumb popped up.

It took less time to cross the border than she expected; the lines coming from Mexico into the US were much longer. She wondered how many of them were headed for California. The border guard looked at her passport, then her face. Mir smiled pleasantly, wondering how much bigger the thing was by now and how fast it was traveling.

Then she was driving, catching glimpses of the ocean. She'd never lived close to the water before, never felt the pull of the ocean like some people. Artie, for instance. Now, of course, she did.

A place with a pool, she thought. Then she'd fill the bathtub - and the Soaker for good measure - and figure out what came next.

The Unseen

Paul Edwards

1

The man behind the stall was short and rotund, with a mop of curly hair and a rounded, pockmarked face. He turned toward Lee who immediately dropped his gaze to the DVDs and Blu-rays on display. *Jeepers Creepers. See No Evil. Saw II. Hostel.*

"Looking for anything in particular, mate?

Lee looked up and Curly-Top grinned enigmatically at him. "Not really." Lee offered a brief, cagy smile. "Just browsing, thanks."

"You into horror movies?"

Lee paused as a gust of wind snatched at his hair. "Yeah. Got anything else? Most of these don't interest me at all."

The man gestured with his thumb toward a white transit parked up behind him. "Got the obscure stuff in there, mate. Wanna look?"

The man rummaged through his pockets before Lee could reply and pulled out his van keys as he shuffled toward the vehicle. He opened the back doors to allow Lee to stick his head in.

On the polythene sheets were rows and rows of DVDs, laserdiscs and videocassettes. "Got a few specialist and collector's editions in there," the man sniffed, smiling and rubbing his hands together.

"Blue Underground. Anchor Bay. Alpha Video. Something Weird Video. Directors like Fulci, D'Amato, Lenzi, Mattei…"

Lee didn't hear, he was too busy examining the videocassettes to listen. *Torture Dungeon* and *Bloodthirsty Butchers* caught his eye and, leaning forward, he quickly snatched them. "How much for these?"

The man took them from him, staring at the backs of the boxes for a while. "These are ultra-rare. Thirty quid for the pair, say?"

Lee frowned. Could he afford to spend the rest of his Job Seekers on a couple of videocassettes?

The man saw Lee was reticent, so said, quickly, "Tell you what. Thirty quid and I'll chuck in a free DVD. Can't say fairer than that, right?"

Lee carefully studied the DVD section. *Zombie Flesh Eaters. Naked Blood. Crazy Desires of a Murderer. Guinea Pig: Flower of Flesh and Blood.* Then he caught sight of himself and flinched.

"What's this?" Lee asked, grabbing hold of the DVD, staring into its mirror-effect case at a ghostly caricature of himself. "There's nothing written on the back. Not even a distribution company or anything. Looks to me like an independent feature, or home movie, maybe."

He pulled the disc out of its case and saw the words *The Black Remote* scrawled across it in black marker. "Never heard of it." He puffed out his cheeks with a deflated sigh. "Got most of the others. Guess I'll have to give this a go, then."

The man licked his lips, passed the videocassettes to Lee and closed the van doors behind him. "You come to Standerwick much?" Lee asked as he tensed against the wind.

The man smiled, shaking his head from side-to-side. "First time, mate. Come from Perranporth, Cornwall." Suddenly, the man's smile faltered and he quickly rubbed his eye with a fist. "The ending's unspeakable," he mumbled, the muscles in his face twitching. "The offerings. The Cult of the Infernal Abyss. *Synchronicity.*" He chuckled and whispered harshly into the wind. "A gate must open."

Lee felt the hairs on the back of his neck stand on end. "Eh?"

"Thirty quid," the man said, sticking out his hand and opening and closing his fingers in an impatient fashion. "Come on, come on. Haven't got all day."

Tia sat hunched on the sofa, watching *Hollyoaks* on their beat-up TV. Lee closed the door behind him and she looked up and around with dark, accusing eyes. "Where have you been?"

He put his bag down on the floor by the coffee table, shrugging at her as he straightened. "Nowhere. Just to the market at Standerwick."

"Buy anything?"

He sucked in a breath. "Only a DVD for a couple of quid." He felt the colour rush to his cheeks. "I'm sticking the kettle on. Want a cuppa?" She shook her head, then muttered something under her breath. "What's the matter?" he asked. "What have I done this time?"

She stormed to her feet, shot over to the video cabinet and snatched open the door. "Do you

154

remember this?" She waved a black and white sleeved Sony videotape labelled *Wedding Day 2007* at him.

A thread of bile rose from the pit of his stomach, and from somewhere far off he thought he could hear screaming.

"I put it on earlier. To show Liam. You know what I got instead of images from our wedding day?" She waited futilely for an answer. "Some *crap* showing a girl getting gang-raped and then shot."

"*Last House on the Left,*" he managed, feebly. "It was showing uncut on cable a few months back. I-I couldn't watch it at the time because we were off out to your sister's, remember? There'd been no blank videocassettes, so I…"

"Can't believe I'm hearing this." She grimaced, baring small, stained teeth. "*That* was our wedding video, Lee. We had footage of Liam taking his first steps on it, too."

She switched the TV off, stomped across the room, and slammed the door on her way out.

Deathly silence descended.

He woke with a gasp, his face greased with sweat.

He'd fallen asleep on the sofa, the television still glowing, flickering, throwing jagged blue light across the walls.

He rubbed at his eyes, got to his feet and shuffled toward the bag full of goodies by the coffee table.

Time for a midnight movie, he thought with a grin.

He'd seen *Torture Dungeon* and *Bloodthirsty Butchers* before, so he decided on the other film, the amateurish looking one.

He stuck the DVD in, set it playing with the remote.

No credits, just a decrepit-looking house on a cliff overlooking a beach.

The sandy coves and wildflower-peppered grasslands hinted at Cornwall, which fleetingly made him think of Curly-Top back on his stall. The camera drifted upwards, where seagulls wheeled above the crumbling manse.

It cut to a darkened room.

A man in a black mask was whispering conspiratorially into the camera. Lee strained to listen, to hear, but the spoken words were difficult to make out. Slowly the camera panned through the rest of the house, revealing long spiralling corridors and rooms thick with shadows and rot.

Lee discerned little in way of plot. When the narrative actually began to run, he witnessed a string of brutal murders, perpetrated by that guy in the black paper mask.

Characters were despatched moments after being introduced – some gaunt-looking guy and his girlfriend were jabbed repeatedly with a spear; a woman with pale-green eyes had her throat cut; a man in a black leather coat had his hands and feet bound by cable-wire and a plastic bag thrust over his head; a girl wearing a combat jacket was stabbed in the stomach repeatedly with a machete and finally, a scruffy-looking male was disembowelled with a butterfly knife. There were no gore effects; the camera always panned away or the screen blacked out before it could get interesting.

Though tired, Lee found himself drawn into the film. The macabre atmosphere sang to him and the acting was of a higher calibre than usual for this type of movie.

The Black Remote (if that was what it was called – there were no credits or title sequences at the beginning or end) had no dénouement; it finished abruptly, right after the bloodless disembowelling and snow filled the screen.

The DVD timer told Lee fifty-nine minutes had elapsed; the film was short and frustratingly incomplete.

He sat there motionless, hands clasped on his knees, trying to take in what he'd seen. It had been amateurish, certainly, and he hadn't felt *scared*. Yet, on some level, the film had successfully managed to disturb him...

He rose from the sofa, made himself a cup of tea. Sat back down and searched IMDB for *The Black Remote* on his computer. No trace. He did a Google search and though he trawled through endless result pages he couldn't find any mention of the film.

The faces of the actors and actresses remained branded in his brain. Their contorted expressions, the panic in their screams...

He rubbed his chin in contemplation. Of course he didn't think the film was 'real', but he typed in '*The Black Remote* snuff movie' anyway into an obscure search engine, then scrolled meticulously through the results.

This time, on the second page, he found what he thought could be a lead – the title to a thread called *The Black Remote.*

The link took him straight to a horror movie forum entitled *Let Them Die Slowly.* The forum wasn't active, had only a handful of members, but the thread was definitely called *The Black Remote,* and there was a single entry from a poster named 'Jan' on it:

Anyone seen a low-budget movie called THE BLACK REMOTE? It's a slasher set in a dilapidated Cornish mansion. Only the heavily butchered version's available, which can be found in the usual black markets across the net.

Lee pondered this for a moment or two, then signed up to the forum. He had to wait an hour for the activation email to come through, he killed the time by surfing other forums as he waited.

Once the mail pinged into his inbox, he logged in and posted on *The Black Remote* thread.

I've seen it. The quality of the DVD was poor and the movie was disjointed and amateurish. I liked the morbid atmosphere, though, and some of the acting was well above average. Unfortunately, the killings occur off-camera, so the film suffered from a distinct lack of blood and gore. The absence of an ending really hurt it, too.

The decayed mansion served as a memorable setting and I'm intrigued by the prospect of an uncut THE BLACK REMOTE – where can I find a copy?

He finished typing, then stared at the screen.

Tia surfaced in his mind abruptly, suddenly.

You know what I got instead of images from our wedding day?

He wondered if she knew he was still down here. She hated him being up so late. He dispelled the thought with a fierce shake of the head and took his empty teacup into the kitchen. His thoughts had already moved on from his wife and were now centring on the prospect of an uncensored version of *The Black Remote.* Some gore and a satisfactory ending would elevate the movie massively, he realised.

When he sat at his computer again, he noticed 'Jan' had responded to his post already.

PM me.

From the post tally next to their avatar (a faceless shadow pointing a video camera at the eye of the beholder), it was only 'Jan's' second post. Yet 'Jan' had responded straight away... which Lee thought really strange.

He clicked out the thread and brought up the members list. Selected 'Jan' and 'Send Private Message'.

Hi. PM as requested.

Lee didn't have to wait long; moments later, he received this:

The most complete version of THE BLACK REMOTE is rare and hard to obtain. However, it does tend to seek out those who are suitable… those who are worthy, shall we say?

"Huh?" Lee shook his head. "What the fuck's that supposed to mean?"

He glanced at the time on his computer. A quarter to five in the morning. "Christ." He vigorously knuckled his eyes. Tia would be up in an hour.

He had to get to bed. And fast.

2

He woke to the sound of rain clattering against rooftiles.

His thoughts were scrambled, drowned in static, like snow at the end of a beaten videocassette.

He stretched out and flung back an arm. Tia's side of the bed was empty. He sat up, gazing blearily about the room. According to the clock on the dresser, it was a quarter to one in the afternoon. *"Shit."* Tia would be at work and was due to finish at four, which meant he had three hours left on his own; Tia's mum was having Liam after school so Lee could job search.

Tia had left him a note and a newspaper cutting advertising for fork-lift truck operators in Westbury,

160

downstairs on the kitchen table. *Saw this and thought of you. Can you pick up bread, teabags and milk at the shop. T.*

Application forms would be going out this afternoon, then the recruitment line would be closed. The job didn't interest him in the slightest, although he knew he had to find work soon; Tia's wage was barely covering the bills and their debts were mounting at a seemingly astronomical rate.

I'll ring the number, he promised, but later – he needed coffee and something to eat first.

He thought back to the message from 'Jan' as he shook cornflakes into a bowl. *The most complete version of* The Black Remote *is rare and hard to obtain.*

He froze and stared glassy eyed at the wall, mulling over those words. Didn't he have a reference book somewhere on obscure movies? He put the cereal box down, dashed upstairs and entered the spare bedroom.

There was a box under the bed filled with old film and horror magazines. *Fangoria. Shock Xpress. Headpress. The Dark Side. Fear.* He rummaged through them, but the book wasn't there. He opened the cupboard where a stack of books and magazines were stored and immediately a book fell and landed with a *thud* by his feet.

He stooped, picked it up.

Suddenly, the reference book fled his mind. He sat on the carpet and flicked idly through the freshly rediscovered photograph album.

161

There were Polaroids of Lee and Tia at parties; on holidays he could scarcely remember; of the two of them at hazily recollected social events.

In each picture he didn't recognise himself – he was smiling, his young face so fresh and alive. There were pictures of their first house together: a three-bedroomed terrace in the centre of Trowbridge. He saw faded photographs of Liam crawling; of his son in a highchair with chocolate smeared around his mouth; of his boy resting upright in the crook of Tia's arm.

The book dropped into his lap and he swiftly covered his face with his hands. Tears slid warm and silent through his fingers, spattering the plastic pockets of the album. "Sorry," he whispered to no one in particular. "So, *so* sorry."

Tia came home after five, tired, cranky and wet. Liam trudged into the house behind her, dropping his lunchbox and bag to the floor, not even bothering to acknowledge Lee as he stomped upstairs to his room.

Lee switched the TV off, then hid his *The Black Remote* DVD behind the sofa. "How was your day?"

She dumped her bags on the carpet, then said with a grimace; "Kids were a nightmare. The weather meant there was no outdoor play, so they've been cooped up inside, driving me to distraction." Tia was a teaching assistant at Roundhill Primary School, a job she disliked immensely. She found each day a struggle and never failed to return home drained. "Honestly

162

thought I was going to lose it with them." She draped her coat over the arm of a chair before drifting silently into the kitchen.

Outside, the unrelenting rain crackled and spat against the window.

"What about the shopping?" she shouted, a short while later.

Lee squirmed in his seat. "Shit. I…"

"Bet you didn't ring about that job, either."

He chewed the inside of his mouth.

"Fuck's sake, Lee!"

He got up, clenched his fists and gingerly entered the kitchen. "Sorry."

"Don't want to hear it. Fuck off." She was sitting at the table, smoking one of his cigarettes.

He couldn't think of anything else to say, he stood staring gormlessly at her for a moment or two. Around him the kitchen darkened as a bare, coffin-shaped room began to superimpose itself over his surroundings…

Tia coughed, snapping him back into the present. "Have you been dipping your fingers into Liam's savings again?"

"What…?" He jumped slightly, mouth gaping open and shut as he retreated toward the door.

Her cigarette was smouldering, her thumb and forefinger almost touching as she lifted her left hand. "I'm *this* close to leaving you right now."

Panicked screams filled his skull and he shook his head to still them. Walk away, he thought. *Just walk the fuck away.*

"You're trying to distance yourself," he said quickly, not really thinking about what it was he

163

was saying. "It's been going on for a while now. You've been turning Liam against me, too."

"How *dare* you!" Tears glistened in her eyes. "The patience I've shown, the chances I've given you!"

He whirled, grabbed his coat from off its hook in the hall. Left the house and slammed the door on his way out. He wandered the estate, muttering, cursing, fists buried deep in his pockets. He didn't want to go back; not until he'd made sense of a few things first.

He began walking in blind circles, occasionally pausing in the street to survey the house. Time dragged, rain seethed. Tia's shadow flitted intermittently past the living-room window.

Eventually the downstairs lights winked out and Lee counted to one hundred before making his move. He took his key out of his coat pocket, unlocked the front door and crept quietly inside. It was obvious Tia and Liam had gone to bed and so with a sigh he hung his coat on a radiator and sneaked off to the living-room to switch on his computer.

He sat at his desk, logged on to the *Let Them Die Slowly* website.

No new messages.

His shoulders sagged.

Just as he was about to log-off again, a message from 'Jan' popped up on screen, throwing him completely.

THE BLACK REMOTE is sufficiently interested in you – you have shown promise, my friend. Keep us in your thoughts, and perhaps it shall reveal itself to you soon.

Lee stared long and hard at the message, then dropped his hands into his lap and hissed, *"...the fuck?"*

Too tired to respond, too exhausted to think up a reply, he switched off the computer and rose wearily to his feet.

He caught sight of *The Black Remote* sticking out from behind the sofa.

I should go to bed, he thought. *Catch up on some sleep.*

Instead, he crouched down and scooped up the film.

Snapped open the case and fed the DVD player the disc.

Darkness reigned.

It was so thick that Lee could scarcely see his hand in front of his face.

Slowly, minutely, his eyes grew accustomed to the gloom. "I recognise this place," he whispered.

He was in a coffin-shaped room with stained walls and a grey, splintered door.

He snatched the door open and stepped out on to his own upstairs landing. He looked back to see the room had changed; was now furnished with a familiar bed, cupboard, dresser, and rug.

He gripped the stair rail and crept hesitantly down into the hall, noticing a bluish light glowing beneath the living-room door. Tentatively, he approached it, freezing as he heard hoof falls and the creaking of floorboards coming from somewhere behind him.

He wheeled.

Darkness – nothing there.

"Christ." Sweating, panting, he grasped the handle and turned it until he heard the *click*. He toed the door open and entered the room.

Positioned at various points around the living-room were wax candles, flames sputtering and hissing in the darkness. They were set up on the mantelpiece, the coffee table, around the TV and stereo system. The curtains had been pulled back from the window, the pane a rectangle of thick and impenetrable darkness.

Sat in an armchair in front of Lee was Tia, her blood-streaked countenance fixed and unmoving, her eyes missing from her face. Those gouged holes glistened obscenely and the smile she wore was the smile of a lunatic.

Liam, clad in a black paper mask, stood to her left, his head slightly bowed, his arms hanging limply by his sides.

Lee stepped into the room.

The boy's head shot up.

"Bywa," Liam whispered.

Lee's eyes flashed open.

"Fuck," he gasped, straightening, hastily wiping a thread of drool from off his chin. *"Fuck!"* His heart thudded and thundered, cold sweat beaded his brow.

The TV was humming and flickering in the corner. He stood, disorientated, then realised he'd fallen asleep on the sofa again.

166

"Dad?"

Lee twitched and whirled toward the voice. Liam, dressed in his Superman pyjamas and cape, was lingering in the living-room doorway. Something like relief flowed through Lee when he saw his boy was unmasked and that his eyeballs were most definitely intact. "Liam, hi. Hi. What...?"

"You were dreaming." Liam tilted his head to one side. "Talking and shouting in your sleep again."

"Was I?" Lee emitted a brittle, nervous-sounding laugh. "You okay? Where's Mum?"

"She's out, remember? Visiting Aunt Trudie. She left early. Didn't want to disturb you."

They were silent for a moment. Then, softly, Liam said, "Mum said to wake you at nine. I've got football practice, remember?"

"I remember."

Liam nodded once, turned, and hurried upstairs to his room.

They left for football practice a short while later.

They scurried through teeming rain, their hoods thrown up, their coats zipped up to their throats. Lee knew it was selfish, but all he wanted was to curl up somewhere and watch movies all day. He tried not to show his resentment, even tried to seem interested in the early stages of the training session.

During a five-a-side match, Liam lingered on the side lines as the other fathers screamed and gesticulated wildly at their sons. He stood hunched

167

and grim-faced, the rain hammering down around him.

In his head, Lee was inside a coffin-shaped room in a dark and decayed mansion…

He rubbed his eyes quickly.

Overhead, apocalyptic clouds gathered into shapes, figures, faces. He felt wheezy and out of breath, had to turn away from the other fathers so that they wouldn't notice.

Was he having a heart attack?

He stumbled into the Sports Hall to get himself some water. He found the fountain and quickly drank his fill. When he re-emerged, moments later, the referee blew for full-time and the two teams trudged off the field toward their waiting parents. Some of the kids went to the hall to shower, but Liam wanted to go home and change.

"Did you see me?" Liam asked, clapping his hands, his mud-spattered face projecting the most incredible grin. "Did you see me score the winner, Dad?"

Lee, unsettled and disturbed, stared blankly at him.

They walked home, neither speaking.

Liam hitched his bag over his shoulder, eyes not leaving the ground. The grin was gone, his metal studs scraping the pavement as he walked. Lee, desperately trying to think of something to say, clutched at his coat and stared long and hard into the middle distance.

They arrived at the house a short while later. Liam took his boots off outside, then ran wordlessly upstairs. Tia – back early from Trudie's – looked up and around at Lee from her chair in the corner. "How was it?"

Liam slammed the bathroom door, and Lee winced.

"Is he okay?" Tia's eyes were hard, wide, and unblinking. "What happened?"

"Nothing. It went well. He scored the winner." Lee purposely changed the subject. "How's Trudie?"

"Fine." Her slender shoulders dropped a fraction. "She's invited us over for dinner tomorrow."

"I can't do that," he said, surprising himself.

Her expression immediately crumpled. "Why not?"

"I-I can't be around people at the moment, Tia. I'm… struggling. Sorry."

For some reason Curly-Top flashed into his mind, grinning that odd, enigmatic grin. Then he was back in the moment when she said, softly, "I don't know what's got into you, I really don't. It's like I don't know you anymore."

Without warning she got up and left the room, leaving him exposed to a stark and uneasy silence.

"I'm standing on the edge of something." The words spewed from his lips like bile. "This is *mine*. Something for me."

He fell to his knees and switched on the TV. Fed the DVD player *The Black Remote*.

That decrepit house loomed. The camera panned down long, eerie corridors.

Shadows moved indelibly in corners.

Curved blades glinted and fell.

During the scene where the fourth victim – the guy in the leather coat – descends into a subterranean chamber, Lee thought he saw a shape in the corner of the screen, a hunched figure with horns sprouting from its head.

Now he was beginning to understand what he liked about the film – you could never trust what it was you were seeing...

The killer stepped out of the darkness with the mask over his face and whispered something – two words – into the camera.

Lee patted around for the controller, grabbed it. Rewound and re-played it.

Coaxed the killer out of the shadows again.

"Asterion House."

There. That was it.

He left the video frozen on that black-masked face, hurried across the room and switched his computer on.

It took searching through endless result pages to find mention of the house and the link took him straight to a website on derelict buildings and abandoned places.

A grainy photograph of *Asterion House* appeared – the same house featured in *The Black Remote*, there could be no doubting it.

There were a few words written about the house underneath the picture:

This dilapidated mansion on the East Pentire headland overlooks Crantock Beach and the Gannel Estuary, which runs from the river mouth in Crantock Bay along the edge of Newquay.

Abandoned during the nineteenth century, little is known about its previous inhabitants, although they were believed to have been a family of influence and high social standing. The last in line was a recluse, who rarely left...

Lee scrolled down to see photographs of some of the interior rooms... and recognised them immediately.

One of the photographs depicted the coffin-shaped room where the characters had met their grisly demises. *So they actually shot the film inside the house,* Lee thought with a shudder.

There was something chalked on the floor in the coffin-shaped room and, by pressing his face close to the monitor, he discerned a five-pointed star inside a circle.

His window closed down suddenly and he was left staring at the desktop. He tried to retrieve the page, but was met with the error message: 'This website is currently not available'.

Muttering under his breath, he logged on to *Let Them Die Slowly* and found a message from 'Jan' in his inbox.

He clicked on it, frowned.

Re-read it with a curious mixture of excitement and disbelief:

You have been invited to a special screening of the most complete version of THE BLACK REMOTE at Asterion House tomorrow evening. I shall meet you outside Newquay Railway Station at precisely 6 PM.

I sincerely look forward to meeting you in person. You are very lucky to have been chosen, my friend.

Lee feigned sleep while Tia got herself and Liam dressed. He didn't stir until he heard the front door slam. Then he got himself dressed, took £25 out of Liam's piggy bank and made the long walk to the train station on the other side of town.

He carefully planned his route by the timetable in the ticket office, boarding his first train shortly before noon. There was just one change at Bristol Parkway, after that it was a straight run, getting him to Newquay at a quarter to six in the evening.

Throughout his journey, his thoughts alternated wildly between Tia and *The Black Remote.* He was excited by the prospect of watching the most-complete version of a movie few had seen before, but that was tempered by the guilt of embarking on the journey in the first place. He'd left a note for Tia explaining all, yet he knew she wouldn't understand; this was something for *him,* something he could finally call his own. Once it was over, he would turn his sole and undivided attention to his family again.

I'll be a better man, he thought. *Like the me in those photographs I found the other day.*

He arrived in Newquay dead on time.

He stepped off the train, took his mobile from his jacket and scanned it for messages and missed calls. Why hadn't Tia been in contact? She must have seen his note by now. He put the phone away just as a hand gripped his arm and turned him.

"You're Lee, aren't you?" He stood facing a man in a shabby grey suit and tie. The man's mouth twitched inside a dishevelled beard. "You've come for *The Black Remote*, right?"

Lee nodded.

"Jan." The man offered Lee his hand, which Lee timidly shook. "Nice to meet you. This way please." Jan turned smartly toward a silver Mercedes parked close to a taxi rank, opening the passenger door for Lee to sidle inside.

Jan slipped into the vehicle, pulled on his seatbelt and started up the engine. "We haven't far to go. Strap yourself in, please."

Jan pulled away and soon they were easing along a quiet coastal road, the car's headlights lancing through the darkness. The night smothered the scenery; there was nothing to be seen beyond the twisting, winding surface of the road.

"I'm glad you liked the film." Jan's deep voice resonated throughout the car, untangling Lee from his thoughts. "It's been such a long and arduous shoot."

Lee frowned and glared at Jan's reflection hovering in the darkness of the windscreen. "Where are we?"

"Crantock." Jan's fingers visibly tightened around the wheel. "We're almost there. The house has stood on the cliff overlooking the estuary for hundreds of years. Used to overlook Langarrow, too."

"Langarrow?" Lee was only half-listening; a remote part of him was desperately trying to make itself heard, instructing him to stop, to turn back, to flee this madness immediately.

"Langarrow used to exist between Crantock and Perran," Jan said with a stiff nod of his head. "Until the sands buried it, of course. Wrath of God, they said." He laughed humourlessly, then said, with a smirk: "Some great men lived in Langarrow. Before the storm it was a city of vice, populated by convicts shipped in or trucked across from less... *tolerant* places. My Master's followers built the house on the cliff overlooking the city and that's how it's survived to this very day. My fellow brethren and I have been ensconced beneath the house for a good many years, working tirelessly to bring our Master's vision to life..."

They were slowing down, pulling up in front of some wrought-iron gates.

Jan cranked the handbrake, then operated the electric window. It slid down smoothly and he reached out a veiny hand to press a button on the gatepost.

With the car idling, Lee gazed at distant lights shimmering like an alien constellation on the horizon. "Holiday parks," Jan sniffed, noticing his interest. "A travesty really, considering what was there once."

The gates shuddered open and Jan released the handbrake. Lee's nose wrinkled as the sulphuric smell of the estuary infiltrated the car; with a grimace he swallowed down his nausea and focused on the windscreen.

Dishevelled trees brushed against the Mercedes. Thorny branches scratched at its roof. The car jolted and shuddered as it passed over potholes, knocking Lee from side to side, Jan's reflection flickering like a trapped frame on a screen before him. Then, rising out of the night, grey stone, rotted wood and cracked tiles became starkly illuminated by the glare of the headlights.

"Asterion House," Lee whispered with awe.

Jan pulled up outside the doors and then cut the car's engine. He jumped out, came round to Lee's side, and opened the passenger door. Lee clambered out, squinting at the house as he straightened.

Wrought-iron balustrades and wooden decking hung broken, twisted and askew. Windows were black, sightless eyes. Unintelligible graffiti scarred the brickwork and the neglected outbuildings around them.

Jan hurried toward the doors, fitted a key in the lock and turned it. "So glad you could join us. Especially tonight of all nights!" He pushed and the doors rumbled ominously open. "January 27th. St Winebald's Day! The perfect time to screen *The Black Remote*, don't you think?" He turned and grinned at Lee before beckoning him in with a finger. "You'll meet the rest of the house later, I promise. But first, let's go enjoy the film, eh?"

Unanswered questions rippled through Lee's mind as he followed the man through the doorway into a cavernous hall. Candles burned in glass jars on rickety tables. Cobwebs shrouded skewed chandeliers. To their right a staircase curled away

175

into darkness; without hesitation Jan ascended, his feet thudding down on the wooden treads.

The stairs led to a darkened landing where an unpainted door awaited. "In here," Jan said, twisting and pushing the handle, "is the theatre." The door opened onto red swing seats and a whirring projector set behind a window in an adjacent wall. The room was only partially lit by the projector's pale-blue glow and a red EXIT sign buzzing on the wall opposite.

Lee felt too on edge to fully appreciate the cinema's dank and decayed charm and so lingered in the darkness for a while, spellbound and silent.

"Take a pew," Jan said and Lee snapped from his reverie as Jan brushed past him to shuffle along the third row of seats from the front. Jan stopped, pulled open a chair and perched himself on it. Lee sat beside him, crushing his hands together in his lap.

A blank screen suddenly filled the wall before them, followed by exterior images of Asterion House. Moments later shots of empty rooms flashed before Lee's eyes. He blinked and looked around curiously, scanning the room for others, but there was nobody here but them.

He grimaced, his eyes flicking back to the movie.

The man in the black paper mask stepped out of the darkness toward the camera, *toward the viewer* and Lee felt himself shudder involuntarily.

The thin-looking male and his dark-haired girlfriend squealed and shrieked as they were jabbed repeatedly with the spear; the woman with pale-

176

green eyes gurgled horribly as blood spurted from her open throat; the plastic, vomit-clotted bag sucked in tight around the young man's face as he fought futilely against his ties; the girl in the combat jacket pleaded convincingly for her life before the machete was plunged into her; finally, the scruffy-looking male emitted a harrowing scream as his belly was slashed, his innards slopping out of that cavity to land steaming by his feet.

Thoughts of snuff movies again surfaced and Lee gripped the armrests to still his trembling hands.

It's not one of those, he told himself. *Just fucking good acting and effects.*

After the final kill, Jan stood abruptly and made his way toward the centre aisle, his seat swinging shut behind him.

Lee barely noticed, his eyes still glued to the screen.

Will I be rewarded with an ending this time? he thought with a frisson of excitement. To his disappointment, the movie blacked out and snow filled the screen, just like it had done on DVD. "Where's my ending?" he whispered, turning in his seat to look about him again.

The chairs were empty; there was no sign of his host.

He left his seat, hurried toward the door they'd entered by. Grabbed the handle and turned it.

Locked.

"Let me out!" he shouted, shaking the handle violently. "Open the *fucking* door!"

No reply.

The projector whirred and the film suddenly restarted, exterior shots of Asterion House giving way to rooms thick with cobwebs, shadow and rot.

Lee made his way over to the EXIT sign, discovering a small door beneath it. He grabbed the handle, throwing one last look over his shoulder as he turned it.

Someone was standing behind the window next to the projector – a tall, stooped silhouette with an elephantine head and torso.

Lee cursed as he stumbled out of that grim auditorium, leaving the door open behind him. He was in a corridor now, narrow and oppressively dark. He slipped his mobile out of his pocket and used its meagre light to see.

In front of him were steps leading down into a deep damp vault.

The door slammed.

He wheeled, hearing a key scrape loudly in the lock. "Hey!" he shouted, grabbing the handle, rattling it. "Let me out! Let me out, you *fuck!* What the *fuck's* going on here, *eh?*" His voice echoed off stone walls and gradually faded to nothingness. With a snort of self-loathing, he vehemently rubbed tears from his eyes and cautiously approached the stairs.

He put one foot in front of the other, descending into a chamber lit by candles in small alcoves. Directly in front of him was a splintered door, hanging ajar as though ready to receive him.

He checked his phone again, considered calling the police. He could alert them to what was going on; direct them to Asterion House and the secret rooms inside it. But as he lifted his mobile, he swore under his breath – no signal here.

A low chuckle.

He spun to see something red flashing in the gloom.

Rather than confront whoever was there, Lee snatched open the door and stumbled into the familiar confines of a cold, coffin-shaped room…

More candles burned and dripped in the darkness, shadows slithering across bare, filth-encrusted walls.

Before him, chalked in red on warped floorboards, was a five-pointed star and around it – within the wide outer circle – were the six victims of *The Black Remote*.

They stood facing one another, frozen at the consummate moment; on the very brink of death.

In the far corner of the room, a group of robed figures whispered amongst themselves as Lee edged nervously forward. He ignored them, eyes locking on the stars of *The Black Remote* instead.

The boyfriend and girlfriend with their torn, ruptured flesh.

The young man with plastic pulled tight around his face.

The woman with the pale-green eyes clutching at her throat.

The girl with the machete embedded in her body.

The scruffy, unshaven male bent over, his stomach eviscerated.

They looked horribly lifelike – too authentic to be anything but… *real*. "My God."

179

He had to at least try and phone the police, try and get help and ,ripping his phone out of his pocket, he saw he had signal at last.

He hit 999 with trembling fingers, but his mobile rang before he could make the call. He held the device up, Tia's number flashing onscreen. He dropped it as he attempted to answer, the phone bouncing, spinning and skittering away across the room.

One of the robed figures snatched it up, candlelight painting the pockmarked face within the hood.

"He's here, with us. The Cult of the Infernal Abyss." Curly-Top pressed the phone closer to his sneering lips. "Thank you for all you've done. The boy, too."

Lee's attention was snatched toward another figure – the black-masked man – who'd stepped out of an alcove and was now wielding a chainsaw in his hands. He was giggling, staring intently over Lee's shoulder at something. "Ready, Master?"

The masked man yanked the chainsaw cord and Lee shrank toward the door, then whirled when he heard hoof falls and the creaking of floorboards.

There was that flashing again – a tiny red dot – and Lee realised he was looking straight into the lens of a video camera.

The operator lingered near the open door, Lee catching sight of fur-lined shins and cloven hooves.

He spun to face the chainsaw again, which had now gunned into life.

"Watch!" the masked man shouted as he raised the saw above his head. "Watch and *marvel,* friend!" He nodded toward the half-dead things positioned around the star. "Bywa!"

Those things instantly came to life, shrieking and squealing in their death throes.

"Rewi!"

The word stilled them, denying them death once more.

Within those ragged holes, the masked man's eyes glared above his saw as he said, loudly, "We're almost there. *Almost.* We've been searching for the right formula for *centuries.* Now it's just you … the last of the seven … and it has to be *simultaneous!* All of you at the same time. To bring this to an end – so that *many* can witness *The Black Remote* in its full and flagrant glory!"

The words barely registered as Lee recognised that deep, booming voice as Jan's. He shook the realisation off and looked for an escape route, but an abrupt swipe from Jan's saw forced him between those half-dead things in the circle. With a cry he attempted to punch the man, but the saw dropped and bit deep into Lee's arm, blood spurting off in all different directions.

The robed figures in the corner laughed pitilessly at his plight.

Above the sound of his own screams, Lee heard Jan shout "Bywa!" and immediately the other victims came to life, shuddering and shaking as they rushed inexorably toward oblivion.

The saw dropped again, ploughing straight into Lee's chest, sending him sprawling to the ground before his attacker's feet.

Jan cut his saw and tore off his mask, his bearded face twitching with delight. "The gate's opening." He turned toward the misshapen figure with the camera. Looked again at Lee and the red pentagram on the floor. "The Spawn of the Abyss will bring blessed insanity to all!" His voice quivered on the verge of hysteria.

Blood was erupting from Lee, his vision fading, breaking, failing. The other victims collapsed like string-severed marionettes, their blood staining the floorboards, their mouths wide and grotesque Os.

The Master cantered forward, camera raised, filming the smoke that was beginning to billow and rise all around them. Suddenly, Jan's eyes bulged and he laughed and screamed all at the same time. The robed figures in the corner began to scream too, raising their hands they clawed frantically at their faces, gouging out their eyes, blood flashing and flickering from out between their fingers.

The Master continued shooting as Lee felt the presence of many begin to materialise around him. And as he tried to turn, to see them, total darkness descended before he could catch so much as a glimpse of his ending.

The Gabbler

Jason R Frei

Bentley sat in the car with the windows up and the air conditioning on full blast. It was hot. Middle-of-the-summer, people-do-stupid-things hot. The coolness of the air conditioning hit the window and created little shimmery waves on the hot glass. People shuffled along the sidewalk slowly with their heads down and shoulders slumped, like zombies. Even the buildings seemed to be wilting and droopy.

Bentley's mop of red hair stuck up haphazardly on his head. Thick, black-framed glasses perched in the middle of his freckled face and magnified his green eyes. He was thin and pale and no amount of sun would ever change that.

He was a bright boy who didn't fit into any sports or clubs and always seemed to be alone. He sat alone in the back of the class. He sat alone at lunch with his bologna sandwich and carton of milk. He sat alone on the playground drawing pictures in the dirt with a stick. And now, he sat alone in the car waiting for his dad.

` Bentley hated being alone. It made him feel incomplete, broken. It reminded him of things he wished he could forget and forget the things he truly wished to remember. Bentley had, as his teachers always said, an overactive imagination.

His thoughts usually kept him good company so he let his mind wander and dreamed up stories in his head. Bentley liked creating stories. Truly fantastic and magical stories. He dreamed of brave knights fighting dragons and evil wizards and rescuing damsels-in-distress. He dreamed of aliens and spaceships and huge intergalactic battles. He dreamed of vampires and werewolves and ghosts and goblins. Sometimes though, when he let his mind wander too far, the monsters won.

Currently Bentley was lost in one of his made up stories. He drew pictures in his notebook, like little comics. His tongue stuck out the side of his mouth when he was concentrating and he held his breath for far too long.

Bentley let out the breath he was holding and looked up to glance at the mouth of the alley across the street. Just inside the alley, mostly hidden by shadows, was a small silver flying saucer. Flashing lights strobed around it in a circle. A ramp slanted down from the bottom of the ship and an alien sat on it. The alien had a green egg-shaped head with large black eyes. A glass dome encased the head, presumably, thought Bentley, so that it could breathe. It wore a silver foil jumpsuit.

Bentley was shocked and he thought the heat was making him see things. People walked back and forth in front of the alley, but none of them so much as glanced sideways at the spaceship. Bentley stared with his mouth open. The little green alien looked up, smiled and waved to Bentley. It got up and went into the ship. It was gone briefly and then returned with an ice cream cone in its hand. It was vanilla with rainbow sprinkles, Bentley's favorite. The alien waved for him to come over.

He was just about to open the car door when his father got in beside him. Bentley was startled and let out a little shriek. His father laughed, not unkindly.

"My goodness, Ben." Only his father called him Ben. "Were you lost inside your head again?"

Bentley quickly looked back to the alley, but it was now empty. He twisted and turned in his seat to look at the sky and saw nothing

"What is it, Ben?"

Bentley opened his mouth to tell his father what he saw, but thought better of it. People already thought he was strange. He didn't want his father to look at him like that too.

"Nothing, Dad. Thought I saw a hawk."

His father ruffled his hair. "You ready to go grocery shopping?"

At that moment, Bentley's stomach let out a large growl. He grinned sheepishly.

"I'll take that as a yes."

Bentley took one last look behind him as his father pulled out onto the road. He thought he saw a silver streak shoot up from the alley to the sky, but it could have just been his imagination or the heat playing tricks on him.

***

A few days later, Bentley sat on a bench in the park. He came to the park often and told his dad he was meeting friends there. He didn't want him to know he had no friends. Dad packed him a sandwich, some cookies and two juice boxes. Bentley munched on the cookies and wrote in his notebook.

It was still hot out, but most of the benches were shaded by the maples that grew in the park. The park wasn't large, but it had a nice-sized walking trail, a playground and a softball field. The first base side of the softball field bumped up against a dense tree line.

Bentley was hunched over his book when he had the sudden urge to look up. Just past first base was a small clearing in the tree line where the walking trail entered the woods. Standing a few feet inside the woods on the trail was a woman. She was very pale, almost white, with sparkling blue eyes. Her hair reached to her waist and looked like it was made of spun gold. She wore a long flowing dress the color of the sky after a thunderstorm, a dark bruised purple. The dress was covered in white pinpricks and sparkled like a star studded night.

Bentley stared in amazement as tiny faces and figures peered out from under and behind the woman's dress. Small, lithe forms with sharp angular faces. Some of them had gossamer wings. The woman saw Bentley staring and laughed a high musical laugh. She beckoned to him.

Bentley was halfway across the softball field before he realized he had left the bench. He was mesmerized and didn't feel in control of his own body, but it wasn't an unpleasant feeling. He was just about to cross the first base line when he was violently tackled to the ground. Someone had him pinned face down and was yelling at him. He struggled for a few moments, but it was futile and he gave up.

"Do you understand me?" It was a gruff voice, a boy's voice.

Bentley grunted and shook his head yes. The grip on his arms was released and he was dragged up to a sitting position. Sitting across from him was an older boy, maybe fourteen or fifteen. His tanned face looked angry. He had menacing brown eyes that matched his scowl. His hair was dark and rumpled, sweaty. He wore a t-shirt and cut-off jeans with sneakers, no socks. He looked at Bentley and thrust out his hand.

"I'm Billy," he said.

Bentley ignored the hand. "Why'd you tackle me?"

"Look, kid," Billy shook his head. "I just saved your life."

Saved my life?" Bentley was annoyed. He never really got angry, but he was close this time. "From what?"

Billy's voice grew quiet, hushed. "From the Gabbler."

Bentley looked back over at the tree line, but it was empty. "What's a… a Gabbler?"

Billy took a deep breath, glanced over at the trees, let the breath out and shook his head. "Not here. C'mon"

Billy stood up and offered his hand again. This time, Bentley took it and stood up. Billy pointed over to the bench that Bentley had been sitting on. "Let's go over there."

Bentley walked back across the softball field with Billy. Neither of them said a word. When they got to the bench, Billy picked up Bentley's notebook and began paging through it.

"Hey," said Bentley, even more annoyed. "That's mine!"

"Did you draw all these yourself?" asked Billy, ignoring the pleas. "Impressive."

"They're my stories," said Bentley, puffing his chest out just a bit.

Billy stopped at one of the pages. It was a new story Bentley had been working on about a boy who was kidnapped by elves and became their king. On the page was a picture of the Queen of the Fairies. Billy turned the page toward Bentley.

"Is this what you saw in the trees just now?"

Bentley looked at his drawing and stammered, "Y-Y-Yeah. That's exactly what I saw."

Billy's voice dropped to a whisper. "It's the Gabbler. It's a monster that looks like the stuff in our dreams."

"Why would it do that?" asked Bentley.

Billy fixed Bentley with a hard stare. "So you would go up to it. So it can snatch you and kill you."

Bentley laughed nervously. "That's crazy."

Billy's mouth formed a tight line and his eyes flashed in anger. "Don't believe me then. Come meet the rest of the gang and hear what they have to say."

Bentley was just a little afraid, of both the story and of Billy. He didn't want to anger the bigger kid, so he agreed to meet the gang. Besides, maybe they would let him join and he could finally stop lying to his dad about having friends.

***

Bentley walked with Billy to Billy's house. He lived toward the middle of the town and wasn't that far from where Bentley lived. Billy introduced Bentley to his mom. Billy and his mom lived alone and they seemed happy. There were several pictures of Billy's dad, but he was not mentioned. Billy took his time showing Bentley around the house. He seemed quieter, more subdued.

When the tour inside was complete, Billy took Bentley to the back yard. It was fairly large, surrounded by a high wooden fence. The grass was green and there were flowers against one of the fence lines. In the middle of the yard was a large old silver maple and nestled in its branches was a treehouse. Bentley had always wanted a tree house; they featured prominently in many of his stories.

The tree house was large, built around the trunk of the tree. It had a wraparound porch and each side had a window. The roof was slanted. Billy said it was so the rain would slide off and not rot the wooden planks used to build the house. A rope ladder was the only entrance to the tree house and led up through the floor.

It was immense. It could easily hold ten kids with room to move around. There were wooden benches on two of the adjoining walls making an L shape, like a sectional. Pillows and blankets cushioned them. One of the walls had a large square painted with chalkboard paint. There were doodles all over it in brightly colored chalk. Posters of cars, sports figures, rock bands and celebrities hung on the walls and ceiling. Several large rugs made up the flooring. The roof had a hatch that could be opened and let the stars shine in on a clear night.

Billy had used his cell phone on the way to the house to text the remaining members of the gang. This consisted of four kids who were waiting inside the tree house for Billy and Bentley. Billy was the unofficial leader because he was the oldest, but only by a few months. Next in line was Samantha. Everyone knew to call her Sam. She was a tomboy through and through. She wore her brown hair short and always had on a t-shirt and jeans. She was also fifteen but acted like she was a lot older.

Veronica was the other girl in the group. She was thirteen with pale blue eyes and long golden hair. She wore a baggy sweatshirt and sweatpants to hide the baby fat that never went away. She liked to smile a lot which showed off the pink and green bands in her braces. She blushed a bit when she was introduced to Bentley and he smiled.

The last member of the group was Freddie. He was twelve, like Bentley. His clothes were worn and had faded stains that even the wash couldn't get out. Freddie's hair was close cropped, like a Marine. He was wary of Bentley, but that's how he was with everyone.

After the introductions, Billy cleared his throat for attention. "Thanks for coming over guys. Bentley and I were at the park today and we saw the Gabbler."

The other members started asking questions one after the other and Billy waved them down. "I'm going to let Bentley tell the story since it's his to tell." Billy sat down.

Bentley told the other kids about the happening at the park and what he had seen. He showed them the drawing in his notebook. He also told them about the alien and spaceship he had seen earlier in the week. He flipped through his book, closer to the beginning and found a picture of a Martian sitting on his flying saucer eating ice cream.

The other kids were quiet and Bentley grew nervous. *Maybe this was some sort of prank*, he thought. The silence continued and Bentley was uncomfortable. He was sure that it was a joke and he just wanted to leave. He was about to say something when Veronica spoke up.

"I saw it the first time at school," she said, head bowed and eyes closed. She cleared her throat and looked at Bentley. "I was the last one in the locker room. I don't like to shower in front of the other girls on account of... well, I just don't. I had just finished tying my shoes when a little yellow and black finch landed on the end of the bench.

"I love birds. My mom and I used to go to the park and try to name as many as we could. This was before my stepdad." Veronica tugged at the cuff of her shirt sleeve, pulling it down around her hand. "Anyway, it was an American Goldfinch. It sat there and whistled at me a few times, like it was trying to talk to me.

"I took a step toward it and it flew up to the locker. I took another step and it hopped back where

I couldn't see it anymore. I went around to the next row of lockers and there was a beautiful Eastern Redbud tree with the most brilliant pink blossoms."

"Wait," said Bentley. "There was a tree growing in the girl's locker room?"

Veronica looked at Bentley with hurt in her eyes. Bentley lowered his head. Veronica was silent for a minute and then started again. "Anyway... there was this tree about as tall as the lockers it was filled with yellow finches. It was the most beautiful thing I ever saw. And then the tree spoke to me."

Bentley opened his mouth, but remembered the hurt look at his last question and quickly shut his mouth. Veronica looked satisfied.

"That's when I noticed a face on the tree trunk. It was wrinkled, like the bark and looked friendly. It said, 'Don't you just love the colors?' It sounded a lot like my Grandpop did when he was alive. Then the tree kind of stretched out one of its limbs and there was a fruit hanging from it. I'd never seen this kind of fruit before, it was green and looked like an emerald the size of my fist.

"'Go ahead' said the tree, so I reached out for it and just before I touched it, I was yanked backwards and pulled around the lockers. That's how I met Sam." Bentley looked between Veronica and Sam without saying a word.

One by one, the rest of the gang told their stories. Sam saw the Gabbler as a svelte Amazonian warrior behind the ice cream shop downtown. "She was like Wonder Woman, but even prettier," said Sam. Billy had saved her by hitting her in the back with a rock and breaking her attention.

Freddie was playing in Jacob's lot when he first saw the Gabbler. Jacob's lot was the parking lot of the old mall which had closed years ago. A small earthquake split the foundation of the mall and tore the parking lot into smaller chunks, like floes breaking from an iceberg. Weeds now choked the lot and Freddie liked to hunt through the tall brown grass. The Gabbler appeared to him as a Nubian queen, her exposed breasts full and round. She wore only a sheer loincloth. He would have gone with her to her kingdom if Billy and Sam hadn't grabbed him and dragged him from the lot.

Billy's story was last, but he had been the first to see it. He was walking home from school one day and saw a shadowy man in a mint condition red Ferrari 250 GTO who offered to take him for a ride. The Ferrari was Billy's favorite car. He was just about to get inside when he glanced at the man from the side of his eye and saw beneath the shadow. What he saw shook him to his core and broke the revelry that the Gabbler had over him.

Billy described what he saw in full detail. The Gabbler was thin and sinewy in a tall lanky frame. Its skin was mottled and stretched over thin hard muscles. The hands stretched out and its fingers tapered to razor sharp claws. The head was smooth and elongated with an oversized mouth full of teeth, too many to fit into a normal mouth. The teeth were all filed to points like needles. The nose was just two slits like black teardrops in the middle of the face. The eyes were a swirling red with three black specks in the middle of each. Black veins crisscrossed the head and body and pulsated to a beat that could be felt, but not heard. When the Gabbler turned to look at Billy, its face and head vibrated, slightly blurring its features and a sound came out of its mouth. Billy tried several times to emulate the sound, but nothing came close. He called it a gabbling sound, like shaking a turkey.

Billy was able to resist and in that moment, he gained clarity over the Gabbler. He closed the car door and backed away. The Ferrari's tires spun, throwing a thick stinking cloud up around it and then it just disappeared. Although the sidewalk was full of people, they kept right on moving like nothing happened.

The gang explained that the Gabbler had appeared to them many more times, always appearing as something that they desired. The image was like a glamour, putting a spell on the person who was the target. It could be broken by looking at it from the corner of an eye, to see its true form, or by someone else physically breaking the connection.

Bentley listened to all the stories without making a sound. He didn't think they were trying to pull a prank on him anymore, but he felt that they may be touched, just a little crazy. But he had seen it too. Did that make him crazy?

It was getting dark and Bentley told the crew that he had to go. He had a lot of thinking to do and needed to be alone. As he was getting ready to climb down the rope ladder, Billy put his arm on his shoulder.

"I know this must sound crazy," said Billy. "Believe me, we've all thought we were going

194

through something once or twice, but we have more evidence. Would you meet us back here tomorrow?"

Bentley thought about this. He still wasn't sure he believed any of it, but here was a group of kids his age who were asking him to come back. What could he say?

***

Billy and Sam were already there when Bentley arrived. They seemed to be in the middle of an argument but stopped as soon as they saw Bentley. Sam pushed passed Bentley and went down the rope ladder.

"Is she ok?" asked Bentley.

Billy stared at Bentley for a moment and then said, "She doesn't think you can hack it."

"Hack what?"

Billy eyed Bentley with an annoyed look on his face. "Sit down."

Bentley did as he was told and Billy reached up into the rafters. He pulled down a large cloth-covered object. Billy carefully took the cloth off as if he were unwrapping a family heirloom. Billy sat next to Bentley and showed him a leather-bound scrapbook.

"This is everything we've been able to find on the Gabbler."

Billy opened the book to page one. Centered on the page was a yellowed newspaper clipping from *The Central News*. It was dated September 1890 with the headline "**FIRE UNCOVERS BODIES**

OF 15 CHILDREN". The story detailed the fire of 1890 that destroyed twelve buildings. One of those buildings was the Chapman Cigar Factory. The bodies were discovered buried in the basement.

The next several pages in the scrapbook showed news stories over the next hundred years of similar gruesome discoveries. The last article was from *The News-Herald* and detailed the finding of twenty-two bodies in 1988 after The Great Fire. All the bodies were of children.

The rest of the book was of drawings. They ranged from simple stick figures to intricate and detailed portraits and scenes. The subject matter was as varied as the quality of the drawings themselves. There were carnivals, circuses, spaceships, dragons, zoos, amusement parks and more. Bentley looked carefully at each one.

Billy flipped to the back of the book to one page that was earmarked. On it was a simple colored pencil drawing of a car, a Ferrari 250 GTO to be exact.

"That one's my picture," said Billy. His finger trembled ever so slightly as he traced the outline of the car. He flipped to the next picture. It was a charcoal drawing of an Amazonian warrior, her sword thrust into the sky in defiance. Next was a redbud tree with perfectly drawn yellow finches. The last picture in the book was a crude drawing of a naked woman standing next to a tiger.

Bentley pulled his notebook out of his backpack. He found the drawing of the Martian eating ice cream on his spaceship and pulled the page from his book. He gave it to Billy whoy flipped to the next open page in the book and taped Bentley's drawing down.

Bentley looked up from his page in the book and realized that the rest of the group had quietly made their way up the ladder and were watching him. He slowly closed the book.

"So, what do we do?" asked Bentley, looking directly at Sam.

Her face softened and she nodded. "We've studied all the news articles and they all have one thing in common. The bodies are always found in the same area."

Veronica pulled out a map that was detailed in marker and masking tape. All the lines converged at the northeast corner of the park. Taped around the outside of the map were smaller, older maps. Bentley looked at them closely. The oldest was a hand-drawn map from 1740. There were few houses and much of the land had been occupied by the Leni Lenape native tribe.

Bentley squinted at the map to try to make out the cramped writing. He used his glasses to magnify the writing and saw the word "cemetery" scrawled in the same spot that the lines converged on the large map. He looked at several of the other maps and was able to piece together that the area where the bodies were found had been a cemetery for the Lenape tribe.

"I think we need to go to the library," said Bentley, looking up from the maps. He pointed at the spot on the large map. "I think that used to be an Indian cemetery."

the wires melted into the darkness. The treehouse expanded to an enormous size.

Veronica was next. Her head lolled as her body rose up, a rictus grin of terror frozen on her face. Freddie rose in the air with his arms and legs twisted at impossible angles to each other. Sam reached out to grab the trunk of the tree and was pulled up so fast, she was momentarily lost in the darkness. When she reappeared, strands of white shot through her hair and her face was painted up like a clown.

Billy was the last to join the mid-air dance. He rose slowly and spun in large looping circles around the rest of his friends. His arc took him within inches of the walls and each time it looked like he would hit a wall, he was jerked upward and missed.

Without any warning, the music stopped with a pop, like a balloon being pricked and the children ceased their frantic movements. They hung limply, swaying softly from side to side. A spotlight came on and illuminated a dark shape in the corner.

A form unfurled itself and stepped up onto a ringmaster's platform, the light following it. The Gabbler rose up to its full height, nearly eight feet. Its flesh was sickly looking and greasy. Patches of off-white like maggot flesh peaked out from under glaring whiteface paint. Blackened veins ran like a roadmap up and down the tight skin.

Its gangly arms stretched to its knees and ended in wicked claws, black with red flecks. The body was thin, emaciated and its bones could be seen tearing through the flesh at certain points. Protuberances thrust out from the elbows, shoulders, hips, knees and heels. The feet, like the hands, ended in blackened talons that clicked on the podium.

The Gabbler's head was stretched, like pulled taffy and sat forward on its wiry neck. The chin came down to chest level. Sharp needle-like teeth lined the enlarged mouth. A constant run of drool dripped from it. Two angled slits sat above the mouth, the flesh quivering and wrinkled.

Its eyes were the color of blood and looked liquid in their sockets. Three small black pupils sat in the center of each eye. There was an ancient bestial intelligence in the eyes. They spoke of ages long past, of the beginnings of the universe, of some horrible deed that had befallen it.

The Gabbler glared at them balefully, piercing their souls to the core. Its thin lips curled up into a hideous smile. Its cruel mouth opened and it screamed, a high pitched, echoing warble. It took one impossibly long step down from the podium and was in front of Bentley. One razor tipped finger reached out and jabbed Bentley in the middle of the forehead. A thin trickle of clear liquid ran down between Bentley's eyes. His head rocked back, his eyes rolled up and his mouth opened in a silent scream.

Images flashed through Bentley's pierced mind. He saw scenes of a Native village. The Lenape hunted and farmed the land, fished the river. He saw their lives and their deaths. The children were buried in their own graveyard, out of reverence.

Years passed and white men came to the land. They struck a bargain with the Lenape and they

200

lived peacefully together for some time, until the land was not enough. The white men drove out the Lenape and took their land. The children's graveyard was first razed, then burned. A manor house was built, which later became a cigar factory and then a silk mill and finally a church.

Each time the land was built up, children went missing and then fire came along, destroying the land and uncovering the bodies of the children. Each time, the Gabbler rejoiced and then retreated to where it had come from.

The Gabbler pulled its arm back and sucked on its finger as it tasted Bentley's essence. Bentley dropped to the ground with a thud. The creature reached out his hand to Sam and before it could touch her, it staggered back and squealed.

Bentley pulled his pencil out of the Gabbler's leg and drove it down again into its foot. The Gabbler lost its control and the other children dropped to the floor. The spotlight snapped off, leaving the tree house in perfect darkness.

A light stabbed the darkness from a flashlight in Freddie's hand. He pulled the rope to open the hatch in the roof and sunlight poured in. The room snapped back to its normal state. There was no sign that the Gabbler had even been there.

Bentley helped the others up. He possessed a strength he did not have before. When he was touched by the Gabbler, he gained something, some primal knowledge. He wasn't sure if it was the knowledge of what he saw, or if it was an understanding of why the Gabbler did what it did. He just knew that he wasn't afraid anymore.

201

He told the others of what he saw when the Gabbler touched him. He described the power that even now coursed through him.

"We could have been killed," said Billy.

"We *could* have been killed," said Bentley, "but we weren't. Right now, we need to find out everything we can. It's the only way to beat it."

Sam coughed and the others turned toward her. "Bentley's right. It could have killed us, but it didn't. For some strange reason, I think it wanted us to see." Sam turned and looked at Billy. "I think we need to go see your uncle."

Billy sighed deeply and scrunched up his face. "Fine," he said in a way that let the others know that it was not fine.

***

Thomas Proudfoot, Billy's uncle, lived on the edge of town. He was Billy's father's brother and not many people ever went to see him. He had been a troublemaker when he was a kid and it had only gotten worse as he grew older. He drank constantly and smoked a bitter and acrid jimson weed that he cultivated in a patch behind his trailer.

His plot of land was more weeds than grass and the children waded through it. It was brown and dry and rustled like paper. They made their way to Thomas's front deck. The trailer was a single and had seen better days. The siding was rusted in spots and green moss crept up one of the corners and spread across the tarred roof. An old Ford pickup sat rusting next to the trailer.

Thomas stood on the deck as if he had been waiting for someone. He was shirtless and shoeless and had on a pair of cut-off jeans. His skin was a deep nut brown, the brown of a man who spent many shirtless days out in the sun. His hair was black and hung down to his shoulders. Thomas had a bottle of beer in one hand and one of his nasty hand-rolled cigarettes in the other. He waved to the children as they made their way toward him. A huge warm smile spread across his face.

"Billy," he said, his deep voice resonated across the gap between them. "I knew you'd be here soon."

Billy mounted the stairs of the deck and gave his uncle a hug. Billy had been very close to his uncle at one point, but had not seen him in some time. Billy introduced his friends and Thomas shook hands with the boys and kissed the girls on the back of their hands.

Thomas Proudfoot was of the Lenape tribe and was a self-proclaimed keeper of their myths and legends. His mother was of the Turtle clan and Thomas had a very large turtle tattooed on his back. In the middle of the turtle's shell was a tree. Thomas pulled out five chairs leaning on the deck's wooden railing and gave one to each of the children. He grabbed his chair and motioned for them to follow him.

The small troupe went behind the trailer to a clearing. A fire pit had been recently set up and was just waiting to be lit. A smoking grill sat next to the trailer, a savory scent wafted from it. Thomas checked on the burgers and hot dogs cooking on the grill. He gestured for the children to set up their chairs around the fire.

"Are you expecting someone, Uncle Tom?" asked Billy. "Did we come at a bad time?"

"A bad time," said Thomas, halfway between a question and a statement. "I suppose it is if you are here, but the five of you are just who I was expecting."

"You were expecting us?" asked Veronica.

"Yes. Turtle told me you were coming and there would be great danger."

Thomas struck a long wooden match off the side of his trailer and lit one of his foul-smelling cigarettes. He then tossed the match into the fire pit and it whoomped into a great fire. It burned blue for just a moment and then returned to its regular orange-yellow-red.

Thomas looked at Bentley and pointed at him. "Turtle told me to listen to you. It said that you have some ancient knowledge that is of great importance."

Bentley told Thomas everything they encountered with the Gabbler, from Billy's first confrontation to their fight in the treehouse. Thomas was given the scrapbook and maps to look over during the long story. At the end Bentley told Thomas about the knowledge he gained when the Gabbler touched him.

Thomas was quiet for a long time after the retelling. He absently reached into a cooler under his chair and pulled out a bottle of beer. He popped the top and chugged the entire bottle without taking a breath. Then he stood up.

"We'll eat first and then find out what Turtle has to say. C'mon."

He put the hamburgers and hot dogs on a platter and set it on a small table next to the grill. There were rolls and condiments, as well as bags of chips and pretzels. Under the table was a tub full of ice. The tops of soda cans rose above the ice. The children heaped their plates and resettled around the fire pit. As they ate, Thomas built a large canvas tent around them. He worked quickly.

When lunch was finished, Thomas threw the refuse into the fire. He called it an offering to Turtle. He then reached back into his cooler and pulled out a Ziploc bag filled with the jimson weed. He took out two large handfuls.

"This will be used to open the door to Turtle's realm," said Thomas, indicating the weeds. "I don't know what we will find, but we must stick together. Billy, take that rope from under your chair and tie us all together around the waist."

Billy did as he was told, starting with Thomas, going around the circle and then tying himself last. While he did so, Thomas chanted. He shook his hands in time with the chanting. The air inside the tent became hot and stifling.

Thomas stopped his chanting and looked around the circle. "Once I throw this on the fire, make sure you breathe deeply and inhale the smoke. That is the way of Turtle."

Thomas shook his hands once more and then threw the whole pile of stinking weeds on the fire. The effect was instant. The fire leapt up and danced around. It cackled like an old witch and turned a

205

greenish hue. The smoke thickened and roiled. The children did as they were told and breathed deeply.

It started with a sound, a soft murmuring, like a gently rolling stream. As it grew louder it became words, unlike any the children had ever heard. It became a hard sound.

The fire was the focal point. It was a large bonfire and was both inviting and distant. Several men dressed in feathers and paint danced around the fire, shuffling from foot to foot. In one moment they were bent over and the very next they stretched back upon themselves, their faces to the sky.

The drums pounded, keeping time with heartbeats, the dancing and the breath of the world. The shuffling-dancing became more frantic, faster. The music and the movement reached its crescendo and an explosion sounded in the background. The chanting and murmuring turned to wailing and screams. Women and children scattered as white men stormed the camp, little puffs of smoke expanding from their rifles and pistols.

Bodies littered the ground and blood ran in rivulets. The blood trickled into the bonfire creating a stench, a stench of death. Shadows crept and cavorted on the thick, black smoke. The whole land was on fire and it spread like liquid. Tents and longhouses burned bright in the night. The fields of corn, beans and squash blackened and shriveled.

A small cemetery erupted into flames as tree bark and grass that lined the graves were quickly engulfed. Gases in the burning bodies caught and exploded. Many of the graves were small and held the bodies of children.

The others looked at the map and all agreed on what Bentley had found. Billy shook him by the shoulders in a friendly manner. Sam nodded and smiled. Veronica gave him a side hug and then turned red and pulled away. Even Freddie was excited and shook Bentley's hands.

As the children celebrated, the sound of music started, imperceptibly at first. It gradually increased in such a way the children did not register it. It was the music from a carousel, very much like the King Arthur carousel from Disneyland, but with a sinister undertone as if the notes were all minor, slightly discordant and sped up.

The children did not realize it, but they were soon dancing to it, their celebration becoming more and more frenzied. Sam was the first one to get a terrified look in her eyes, the whites showing more than the brown. The more she tried to stop, the more her limbs flailed like a marionette with a spastic puppeteer.

Shadows and light splayed across the walls of the tree house, imposing dark images, like witches dancing around a bonfire or cannibals preparing a stew. Billy cried out when small pinpicks appeared on his arms and blood trickled out. Soon, the others had similar marks and small droplets of blood spattered the floor.

The music became faster and faster and, when it reached its crescendo, Bentley screamed out as his body lifted off the ground. Black wire strands exited the holes in his arms and reached upwards. The roof of the treehouse was lost in pitch dark shadows and

The village was destroyed and burned to the ground. What was once a vibrant community was now ash, soot and dust. One woman walked alone through the village. She held a small bundle of charred blanket and bones, crying softly. She dropped to her knees in front of the remains of the bonfire.

"Kishelemukong," she shouted as she raised the bundle to the sky. "Grant me my revenge!"

She threw the remains of her child into the bonfire, then streaked her face and arms and bare breasts with the ash and soot and dust of the village. She picked up large handfuls of debris and shoved it into her mouth, choking as she swallowed what remained of her village.

The sky darkened and thunder boomed. Flashes of lightning rippled across the sky. Twin bolts of lightning crashed down and struck the bonfire, lighting it anew. The bundle of bones vaporized into smoke that tendriled out and entered the woman's nostrils. She breathed in deep and as she did, she changed. Her body shifted under its skin. Bones popped and stretched; muscles grew hard and long. She shrieked, a high piercing sound that split the night. The ash and soot and dust mixed with her tears and discolored her body. Joints cracked and splinters of bone split the skin and hardened to spikes. Her eyes rolled up into her head and turned as red as the blood that ran through the village.

Then she stood, looked up at the sky and smiled a fearsome and dark toothy smile. She bounded to the small graveyard and entered an open grave, slipping deep beneath the dirt and into the earth.

***

The smoke cleared the tent as the fire sputtered and went out. Thomas opened his cooler and took out the last two beers. He poured the ice and water on the remains of the fire, as well as the beer, causing one great billow of smoke to fill the tent and rush out into the late afternoon air.

The children woke from their daze as if they had slumbered. Thomas left the tent and began breaking it down. He was sober and would remain so for the rest of his days. A pure white streak ran through his dark hair and his eyes looked haunted.

"What happened, Uncle Tom?" asked Billy. "What did we just see?"

Thomas straightened up. He was facing the back of the property, away from the kids. When he turned around, there was grimness to his face, not determination, but resignation.

"You saw what Turtle had to show you," he said. "The Gabbler is protecting its people."

Sam shook her head. "There aren't any people left for it to protect. It's just out for revenge."

Thomas fixed Sam with a hard stare. "Just let it go, girl. There are things in this world that you shouldn't tamper with."

"But it's killing children," said Bentley. "And I think it has been for a long time."

"Longer than any of us have been on Earth," said Thomas. He looked at his old, dirty hands. His eyes were tired. "How are we supposed to stop it?"

Bentley walked over to Thomas and put his hand on his arm. "You aren't supposed to stop it." Bentley looked at his friends. "We are."

Thomas's shoulders shook as he began to sob. He dropped to his knees and the children went to him and held him. When he was finished, Thomas stood up.

"Where's the map?"

Veronica went to her backpack and handed the map to Thomas. He set it on the condiment table.

Then he tapped on the map where it was clear of tape. "This is the large park near the center of the town. The park stretches for miles. The whole system is actually composed of three smaller parks." He tapped the upper left side of the map, where the lines converged into a point. "This is the oldest park of the three. This is where the cemetery was."

Thomas looked up and pointed across the back of his land toward a tree line. "It's right over there behind the trees."

After saying their goodbyes, the children packed up their bags. They walked home, devising a plan. They would meet at Thomas's house and venture to the park through the back of his property. They were children; they didn't question their plan. They were invincible and everything would work out.

***

Bentley arrived first at Thomas's house. He propped his bike up against the wooden porch and

209

went up the stairs. The screen door on the trailer was closed, but the inner door was slightly ajar. Bentley knocked on the screen door. There was no answer.

A crow called from the maple tree in the front yard. Bentley looked up at the tree which was black with crows. They hopped from side to side on their branches, their feathers and feet making small, whispered noises. Bentley turned back to the door and knocked again.

"Hello? Mr. Proudfoot? It's Bentley."

The trailer was quiet. Another crow cawed. And then another and another until the whole tree was alive with the sound of the crows. Bentley grew nervous and knocked on the door again. Still no answer. Bentley opened the screen door and pushed the inner door open.

"Mr. Proudfoot? Thomas? I'm coming in."

Bentley walked inside. The trailer was as small on the inside as it looked on the outside. The sink had a few dirty dishes, but overall, the living area was clean and tidy. A small television sat on the square kitchen table. Toward the back of the trailer was the open bedroom, which was really nothing more than a bed, a small dresser and a small table with a lamp on it. Thomas was nowhere to be seen.

Bentley listened and realized that he couldn't hear the crows anymore, but he heard the sound of running water. He went to the bathroom door and knocked.

"Mr. Proudfoot? It's Bentley."

He thought he heard a gurgling sound, but immediately dismissed it. He turned from the door and heard a soft click of a lock and the door opened just a crack. Bentley turned back. He heard the gurgling sound again.

Bentley pushed open the door and found himself standing in the bathroom from his own home. The curtain was closed on the tub and the water was running. Bentley remembered this similar scene set out a few years ago. Water dripped down the side of the tub and began pooling on the floor. His hands shook as he pulled the curtain back.

The water filled the tub to the brim and was stained a dark red. Small ripples cascaded across its surface. Bentley was transfixed by the scene. When he was seven, he walked into his parent's bathroom, looking for his mother. He had found her in the tub, her skin white and pruned. She had a gash on each wrist and red-tinted water had overflowed, spilling onto the floor.

Bentley's breath came in ragged gasps and his lips trembled. Tears threatened to spill from his eyes. Suddenly, a hand shot up from the water. The skin was white and almost translucent. A vicious gash tore through the wrist, the flesh around the wound tinged blue. The fingers were wrinkled from the water. A gold ring encircled the third finger.

Bentley screamed and ran from the bathroom. He bolted through the door of the trailer and ran straight into Sam, knocking them both to the ground. The crows lit from the tree in one mass, blocking out the sun momentarily, like an eclipse.

"What the hell, Bentley?" said Sam, picking herself up.

211

Bentley drew his knees deep into his chest and began rocking. He hummed a soft tune with his eyes screwed shut tight. The other children huddled around him asking questions and shaking his shoulders.

"Step back," said Veronica. "Give him some room."

The other children stepped back. Veronica sat down on the porch next to him and put her hands on his knees. She rocked gently with him. After a few moments, Bentley's rocking subsided and he opened his eyes. He looked straight into Veronica's eyes. She smiled gently at him.

"Can you tell me what happened?"

"The bathroom," said Bentley. He tried to say more, but couldn't.

Freddie went into the trailer alone. He returned after a minute. Billy looked at him questioningly, but he shook his head and shrugged.

"There's nothing there," said Freddie.

Bentley's mouth hung open. "But she was there, my mother, just like when I found her."

"Sorry, Bentley, but the bathroom's empty," said Freddie. He held up a gold ring. "The only thing in the tub was this."

Billy turned the ring over several times and then squinted at something. Inscribed on the inside of the ring were the words "Always and Forever". He told the others.

Bentley moaned quietly. "That was my mom's ring. It was their vow."

Billy dropped the ring and it bounced twice, then slipped through the floorboards of the deck.

Freddie went under the deck to look, but no trace of it could be found.

Sam held her hand out to Bentley. "Come on. We'll go in and check together."

Bentley nodded his head and took the offered hand. Sam took the lead with Bentley behind her. Freddie was right. The bathroom was empty. Not just empty, but clean. No murky water filled the tub and the floor was bone dry.

"Where's my uncle?" asked Billy.

"I don't know," said Bentley, finally finding his voice. "It was empty when I got here." He then told them what he had seen. He also told them of his mother's suicide years before. Veronica held his hand and squeezed sympathetically.

The children went out the door and around to the back of the trailer. A fire smoldered in the pit and Thomas sat in a chair with his back to the trailer.

"Uncle Tom?"

The children walked around the chair and let out a collective gasp. Thomas sat rigid in the chair, one arm pointing to the trees he had identified the day before. His face was bloodless, lifeless. His eyes were missing and only dark empty sockets remained. His clothes were covered in ash and soot and dust. His shirt was open, and in ragged lacerations on his chest were the words "Come to me".

Billy was furious and tears streamed down his cheeks. "This ends now."

***

213

The park was only five acres, but on late summer afternoons, it was filled with people. The main attraction was the swimming pool, but that was not where the children were headed. The oldest part of the park was where the Carousel was. The Carousel was built in 1892, almost two hundred and fifty years after the land was taken from the Lenape. The lines on Veronica's map all converged at the Carousel.

It consisted of thirty-six horses and two carriages. The wood frame was faded yellow with green accents. The horses were in varying states of yellow and white with garish pink, blue and red saddles. The eyes of the horses were wide and bright white as if they had been startled.

The center of the Carousel was a thick wooden beam surrounded by a small, enclosed box called the dog house. This is where the original organ was still held and where the children headed.

The Carousel was closed most of the year, only opening on special occasions. The children crossed over the wooden floorboards to the center. There was a door with an antique metal clasp, probably the original. Billy flipped up the latch and opened the door.

It was dark and the children huddled just inside the door. Freddie was the last to enter and as he did, a huge gust of wind sprang from out of nowhere and slammed the door shut, cutting off all light. Freddie turned and reached out to push the door open, but his hands found nothing. He took a few steps forward, but still only groped air.

Sam turned on her flashlight and a thin beam of light stabbed the darkness. Gone were the walls and music of the Carousel. Instead, the children found themselves in an underground cavern. The floor was dirt and rock. Somewhere, high overhead in the dark, was a ceiling. Sam aimed the flashlight up and the end of the beam caught the point of a crystal stalactite. The crystal took the weak beam and amplified it, causing the cavern to light up.

The ground was littered with the bruised and broken bodies of babies. Not children, but babies. They were in varying stages of development, some no more than the size of a lima bean, the features unrecognizable. Others were much more infant-like and fully formed. The floor glistened with bodily fluids. Blood, amniotic fluids and urine mixed together to form a gore-splattered still life.

The children trudged carefully through the mess. Near the middle of the cavern, fat, soft limbs reached out and grabbed at their feet. Masses of fresh pink and decayed white grubbed across the floor. Toothless smiles turned up at them and the sound of cooing and gurgling filled the cavern.

Freddie screamed as a half-formed fetus latched onto his pants and began crawling up his leg. He thrashed wildly, kicking his legs out to detach the grotesquerie. Veronica felt something dribble down the back of her neck and she looked up. The ceiling was covered with more dead babies. She knew instinctively that these were babies that had never been born. Some bore the marks of their stillbirth, holes puncturing brains and hearts. Others had cords wrapped tightly around the necks, their blue faces gasping for air.

Veronica shrieked, a fierce and primal sound which set the entire cavern in motion. The babies crawled furiously as the children ran deeper into the cavern. Billy slid on the gore underneath and fell to the ground. Bentley stopped and helped him up as a wave of fetuses crashed down on them, driving both of them down. The other children doubled back to help and were similarly thrown to the ground. The tiny, greasy bodies crushed them under their weight, as if they were an ocean, drowning the children.

Sam lost her flashlight and the luminescence winked out, rendering the children into darkness again. They clawed and scraped at the crushing mass. Veronica reached out and found Bentley's hand. She gripped it tight and pulled him toward her.

They fought their way together and one by one found their friends. As their hands clasped, the shifting pile settled. Billy pulled out his flashlight and switched it on. The cavern immediately illuminated again.

The children were prepared to dig their way out of tiny corpses, but instead found that they were buried together in loose dirt. They were in an ancient graveyard, no longer inside a cavern. They were now outside, under a gibbous moon. The silvery light stabbed down through rolling banks of smoke. Fire licked at the edges of the graveyard and the orange glow melded with the silver of the moon to create an eldritch effect.

The children pulled themselves out of the ground and explored the graveyard. The graves were unmarked and appeared as small grassy mounds. Some had flowers on them, the stems twisted together. The petals wilted from the heat of the fires. Other graves were marked with small rocks, or pieces of carved bark, or long grasses woven together into dolls.

At the edge of the graveyard was a lone uncovered grave, a mere hole in the ground. The children formed a ring around it. A bundle of rags lay inside the hole. A small skeletal hand peeked out from the bundle.

"I remember this from the vision we had," said Billy. "I think this is the child the woman sacrificed to become the Gabbler."

"I've been thinking," said Sam. "When we each saw the Gabbler for the first time, it took the form of our dreams, our desires. What if we force it to take the form of something we can capture?"

"How?" asked Bentley.

"I've seen your drawings," she said. "I think you could do it."

"But what would I draw?" asked Bentley fearfully. "What could I possibly draw that would give us a chance?"

Veronica took Bentley's hand in hers. "You're smarter and more talented than you think," she said. "I believe in you."

Sam crossed to Bentley and took his other hand. "I believe in you too."

The other boys each came over and put their hands on Bentley's shoulders and back. "We all believe in you Bentley," said Billy.

Just then, a high keening wail started from the other side of the cemetery. "She's coming," said Sam. "We'll distract her while you draw."

Bentley dropped into the shallow grave and took his pencil and notebook from his backpack. The rest of the gang picked up whatever they could find to use as weapons. Veronica turned to Bentley and blew him a kiss before she ran into the heart of the cemetery with the others.

***

The small group formed a line as they ran toward the Gabbler. She met them halfway across the graveyard, her lean body loping across the ground. Billy skidded to a halt and threw the rock in his hand, his ability honed from years of skipping stones across the lake. His aim was true and the flattened rock struck the Gabbler above her eye.

She dropped to a crouch and raised her clawed hand to her head as she let out a piercing howl of pain. A trickle of crimson dripped down into her eye. She shook her head and glared at Billy. Her body launched at the boy like an arrow, outstretched claws aiming for his throat.

Her body was slammed to the ground by the downward swing of a large tree branch in the hands of Freddie. Before she could recover, Freddie began raining blows down on her. In his assault, he got too close and the Gabbler thrust out an arm that took

218

Freddie's feet out from under him. She pounced on him like a cat playing with a mouse. Her taloned arm swiped across his chest, slicing open the shirt and the skin beneath it.

As she raised her claw for another attack, Sam fired a rock of her own that distracted the Gabbler more than it damaged her, but it was enough for Freddie to wriggle himself out of her way. The Gabbler rose to its full glory and began walking toward Sam, a rictus of hate on her face. Freddie swung his branch again, but the Gabbler was ready this time and she snatched it from his hands. She snapped it in half like it was a popsicle stick and threw the pieces over the heads of the boys.

She continued walking toward Sam who turned to run and tripped over an exposed root in the ground. She flipped over just as the Gabbler reached her. The Gabbler smiled its infernal smile and it crouched down again. One lanky arm reached around Sam and gripped her by the back of the head. The Gabbler's head tilted to the side and it stood up, lifting Sam's feet off the ground.

The Gabbler's mouth opened impossibly wide and the stench of death wafted from its maw. Sam gagged and struggled, but the Gabbler was too strong. The Gabbler began to inch Sam's head closer to its mouth. Veronica screamed a war-cry and thrust out her branch, piercing the Gabbler through its side.

The Gabbler let out a roar and flung Sam aside like a rag doll. It shrieked, grabbed the branch coming out of the front of her and yanked it out.

Veronica started running before the Gabbler could turn around, but it was hot on her trail in an instant. The Gabbler bounded close enough that it swung out a narrow arm and knocked Veronica into a fresh mound of dirt. The Gabbler leaped onto her back, driving the wind from her. There was an audible pop as one of Veronica's ribs snapped.

The Gabbler gibbered as a filthy drool slavered from its cruel mouth. A black pointed tongue ran over its lips.

"Stop!" shouted Bentley as he rose up from the grave he had been hunkered in. The Gabbler's head whipped to the side, taking him in.

"Leave her alone," he said, a dark and hard edge to his voice.

Bentley crawled out of the pit and walked toward the Gabbler. The Gabbler's face scrunched up in confusion and it stepped off and back from Veronica. Bentley walked up to Veronica's still body and knelt beside her. He swept the hair back from her head and whispered into her ear.

"I'm here," he said. She stirred and Bentley helped her up. Her face was smudged with dirt and blood dripped from her forehead. He pulled a handkerchief from his back pocket and gave it to her. She looked at him.

"My dad told me that a gentleman always carries a handkerchief in case a lady needs it. Now I know why." Bentley smiled, a warm and genuine smile meant just for Veronica.

The Gabbler made a noise and Bentley turned back toward her.

"You should be ashamed of yourself," said Bentley, as if he were talking to a small child.

The Gabbler chuffed and took a step toward Bentley. He put his hand up and stopped her.

"These are my friends. I'm sorry for what happened to your village and people, but we had nothing to do with it."

Bentley scowled at the Gabbler. "You have killed too many people and it hasn't brought your child back, has it?"

The Gabbler took another step toward Bentley, menace on its face.

Bentley let out a small breath and shook his head. "Just stop. You have no power over us anymore and I'm not scared of you. You're nothing but a tired old dog."

Without a sound, the Gabbler lurched forward and knocked Bentley to the ground. The air was knocked from his lungs. The creature grabbed Bentley by the leg and dragged him closer until it was right over top of the boy. The Gabbler's face split with a maniacal grin. It raised one hand and flicked a razored finger out.

Bentley cowered under the beast and raised his smudged notebook over his head. The Gabbler made to knock it away and then stopped. The outstretched claw touched the paper and traced an outline. Its other hand reached down and took the notebook.

Bentley slowly crawled out from under the distracted creature. He placed the bundle of bones from the grave in front of it. The Gabbler snuffled the rags, sat down and let out a small, lonely howl.

Bentley put his hand on the Gabbler's head and then stood up and stepped back to his friends.

The Gabbler bowed its head to the picture. It lay down on the ground with the picture and the bones underneath its bulk. Its body shook as it transformed again. The form stretched and in place of the creature was now a woman. Her body was tanned and young. Her face was covered in soot and a white paste covered her hairless body.

She sat up with the bundle in its arms. A cry issued from the bundle and the woman smiled. She looked up at Bentley with a tear in her eye and bowed her head slightly. A fog rose up suddenly and swallowed the woman. It swirled around the children and when it dissipated, that place and everything in it was gone.

***

The door of the dog house opened and five dirty, battered children emerged into the Carousel. They trod across the floorboards and into the sun of the day. Someone shouted from across the way and a surge of people rushed toward the children.

Emergency services, reporters and police mobbed the children. Veronica and Freddie were separated from the group and rushed to ambulances to be tended. Attempts were made to interview the children, first by the police and then by reporters. The children said only that they had been chased by some bullies onto the Carousel and had been locked inside.

After some time, the children's parents were allowed to take them home. Veronica suffered a broken rib and two large foot-sized bruises on her back. The slash wounds across Freddie's chest were a little worse and needed several stitches. He showed them off that summer whenever he could.

A few weeks later, the children were allowed out of their respective houses and they met at the treehouse. Veronica's rib had healed enough to allow a tight hug from the others. Bentley hugged her the tightest and even kissed her cheek. She only blushed a little this time.

It was Billy's mom who had called the police. When Billy had not come home for dinner, she got worried and drove to Thomas's trailer. The trailer was empty and there was no sign of Thomas or the children. She was afraid that Thomas had finally snapped and taken them. A search party was organized immediately. To the children, it had felt like only a few hours, but they were missing for a day and a half.

During the course of the search, police found the mangled bodies of two children in the woods surrounding the park. Over the course of the next few hours, no less than fifteen corpses were found, all children ranging in age from five years old to sixteen. Shortly before the children emerged from the carousel, the horribly disfigured body of Thomas Proudfoot had been found.

Sam had dutifully clipped each newspaper article and handed them to Billy to put in the scrapbook.

"It's over," said Billy. "I don't think we need this anymore."

Sam shook her head. "These children died like all the rest. It's only proper that they get a place in the scrapbook."

Billy looked around the group and the others shook their heads in agreement. He put them in the scrapbook. He was about to close the book when Bentley spoke up.

"Wait. I have one more thing for the book."

Bentley produced a folded up piece of paper. It had scorch marks on it and smelled of smoke and dirt. He unfolded the paper and smoothed it out.

"Is that the picture you drew?" asked Veronica.

Bentley nodded. "After I got home, I found this in the pocket of my jeans. I think it was her way of saying thank you."

Billy took the picture and put it in the book. Then he got out his cell phone. "I think it's only right that we finish the book with a picture of us, the ones who survived."

The kids gathered together and Billy took their picture. He showed it to them to get their approval. Centered right behind them was an Indian woman with a baby in her arms. She was smiling a calm, peaceful smile.

Meet the Authors

Paul Edwards is a life-long horror fan and writes his own twisted tales in any spare time that he can grab. He has seen three collections of stories published – *Now That I've Lost You* (Screaming Dreams), *Black Mirrors* (Rainfall Books) and *Night Voices* (Demain Publishing), the latter being a joint-collection with author Frank Duffy. Paul is also a fan of role-playing games, rock music and rough Somerset cider.

Jason R Frei lives in Eastern Pennsylvania where he works as a therapist with children and adolescents. He writes speculative fiction culled from the experiences of his life and those he works with and blends science fiction, fantasy and horror into new creations. His flash story "The Garden" will be featured in the horror anthology *99 Tiny Terrors* by Pulse Publishing and his short story "Some of the Parts" will be featured in the horror anthology *Toilet Zone 3: The Royal Flush* by Hellbound Books Publishing. Visit him online: https://facebook.com/odinstones.

Edward R. Rosick is an author living in the urban wilds of southern Michigan. He has attended both the Taos Toolbox and Clarion Writer's Workshops and his stories of horror and speculative fiction have appeared in numerous magazines and anthologies, including Pulphouse, Sick Cruising, and The Half That You See. His first horror novel, entitled Deep

Roots, is scheduled to be published by Thurston Howl Publications.

Sandra Stephens is a writer living in the Pacific Northwest with her husband and chocolate Labrador, Jake. She has published several shorts in the horror genre, and while she doesn't always write horror, she likes to imagine the most horrific turn of events in any circumstance, making her an excellent dinner party conversationalist.

SJ Townend hopes that her stories take the reader on a journey to often a dark place and only sometimes back again. SJ won the Secret Attic short story contest (Spring 2020), has had fiction published with Sledgehammer Lit Mag, Hash Journal, Ghost Orchid Press, Bandit Fiction, Black Hare Press, Black Petals Horror Magazine, Ellipsis Zine, Gravely Unusual, Gravestone Press, Holy Flea, Horla Horror and was long listed for the Women on Writing non-fiction contest in 2020. She has also written and self-published two dark mystery novels, both of which are available to purchase on Amazon: (Tabitha Fox Never Knocks, Twenty-Seven and the Unkindness of Crows). Follow her on Twitter: @SJTownend